CHRISTMAS

DOINGS

I0619382

MariaLisa deMora

Edited by Hot Tree Editing

Copyright © 2018 MariaLisa deMora

All rights reserved. This book or any portion thereof may not be reproduced or used in any manner whatsoever without the express written permission of the publisher except for the use of brief quotations in a book review. This is a work of fiction. Names, characters, places and incidents are either the product of the author's imagination, or are used in a fictitious manner. Any resemblance to actual persons, living or dead, or actual events is entirely coincidental.

First Published 2018

ISBN 13: 978-1-946738-20-2

DEDICATION

Because creating a found family
can be frightening as well as freaking fabulous.

CONTENTS

ACKNOWLEDGMENTS

When I decided on the idea of writing another holiday novella for our RWMC family, I was pretty darn eager. I've had such fun with them in the past, shining light on the day-to-day lives of some of our favorites, and couldn't wait to see which couple came forwards to tell me their Christmas story this year.

The ones who kept circling back in my mind were two people who so deserved to have a great Christmas. From the beginning, Ester was entirely on board with the idea, chattering away about the pups and tiny humans, but she and I had to talk Bones into taking the ride with us. He can be a grumpy Gus when he doesn't want to cooperate, but he eventually came around and I found his voice again.

Since this is a story released around the Christmas holidays, I was looking for something sweet and precious, a book that would warm people's hearts, and make them smile. Perhaps an extension of the tale from Bones and Ester's original holiday season when he quickly discovered how doings were the most important in the history of everything for her.

I didn't get that at first. Instead, once we got past the funny feathered friends and puppies, Ester steered me down a path that resonated with pain, so much dark flickering with only brief flashes of happy mixed into the story. That was our Ester all over, just keeping it real for me as she is wont to do, and making me dig deeper, even for a holiday novella. She's ever been one to require greater effort, and I think this story is well worth every sleepless night spent in crafting it. It comes out right in the end, I promise you.

If you've read the other stories, you already understand her pain. But, if you've seen the cover, you should know this book holds the best of all possible HEAs. Because, truly, is there a better kind of holiday story than one of true love? And puppies, we can't forget the puppies!

In this holiday season, I want to send out a heartfelt thank you to every parent who puts their child first, whether adopted, fostered, or natural. Within the lives you shelter, you are molding the future, and the tiny humans you nurture and love will someday rule the world. That's a heady responsibility, but I have faith you're up for it.

Ester and Bones might be my favorite couple in the history of ever, and I'm honored they've chosen me to bring their tale to you. Merry Christmas, Happy Holidays, and the Best of Joyous Doings to you all.

Woofully yours, and with so much love,
~ML

Chapter One
Bones

Emilio Salvador de Villa Ramos looked through the windows of his kitchen and out towards the medium-sized backyard. He'd owned the house for years and knew its unique features like the back of his hand. After so long, even he had become a fixture in the community. The longsuffering neighbors had come to anticipate the unexpected from him, and his frequent guests.

Bones, as he was best known in his world, had a habit of looking into the backyard at this time of day. Just home from his job overseeing the roster of mechanics at a local exclusive motorcycle shop, he leaned a hip against the counter near the door. He stared, shoulders dropping an inch as he relaxed for the first time that day. He pulled in a deep breath and fixed his attention on the woman who was carrying a pair of buckets, fussily tending a grouping of unique, creative bird feeders and baths.

My Ester.

He smiled as he noted the new feeder she'd added at some point in the past week. The ornate, refurbished lantern was eclectic and uncommon, and fit right in with the rest of her collection. There were flat platforms balanced on metal sculptures, and those stood beside elaborate, multilevel gravity feeders made from antique stained glass. Each was as individual as Ester herself.

She glanced up and caught sight of him, giving him a view of her wide smile as she carefully set a bucket down and waved vigorously. With broad gestures, she wordlessly asked if he wanted to come outside. Bones shook his head from side to side and laughed aloud when she pretended to pout. He wrapped his arms around himself and shivered with dramatic flair. Waving her hand around, she looked to be conducting a symphony, calling upon one section after another to give up their talents at her whim. With the eye-rolling at the end, he knew she was most likely talking to him. She would be extolling the virtues of their garden, currently covered in about a foot of snow. Still shaking her head, she flipped a dismissive hand his direction before bending back to her task, and he watched with amusement as two birds landed on her hat, as impatient as he was for her to be done.

Her feathered friends were vocal and demanding, but loyal Ester was more than up for the challenge of keeping them fed and watered through the winter months, no matter how much ice and cold Old Man

Winter threw their direction. *She's always been like that*, he mused. Strong and loyal, dedicated to her cause.

Their third Thanksgiving together had come and gone, and they had celebrated as he wanted, he and Ester sharing the holiday with a few select men he called brother, accompanied by their significant others. She'd applied the same traits that made her a devoted caregiver for the birds to the gathering. That meant she'd thrown herself into the planning of the day, beginning with the tray of pancakes she'd made and brought back to bed in time for them to watch the parade on TV. She hadn't considered that pancakes came with syrup, so for a time, there was no thought given to the TV, to the celebrities or floats. Balloons, large and small, went past the cameras, and all he could focus on was sipping the sweetness from her body.

So the holiday had started in great form and continued as their guests had arrived.

Their guests, and their children.

The children had been both the best and the worst of that evening. Ester had gone over the guest list with him dozens of times. She'd asked question after question, quizzing him and making certain she knew even the smallest detail about each attendee. She'd learned names and jobs, and how long they'd been in the motorcycle club of which he was a member and Chicago chapter president, the Rebel Wayfarers MC. Based out of the Mother chapter, most of the men had been to Bones and Ester's home before. Singly or in pairs, but seldom before in a large group. Beginning with confirming their

3

visitors were known and well-tolerated by Ester, Bones had tried to ensure there would be no surprises to trip her up.

He smiled, still watching out the windows. She was on the move, bucket swinging wildly, and he sighed, chuckling softly. The sight of Ester tromping through the garden in oversized galoshes, knees raised high to keep snow from spilling down into the tops of her boots, was enough to lift his spirits no matter the kind of day he'd had. She was followed by a grouping of birds, the tiny winged creatures staying up with her by hops and wing flaps across the crust of the snow, and he imagined they chattered to her with peeps and cheeps. Like chicks. Baby chicks, following their mother.

He sighed deeply, pulling in a big breath and holding it for a moment before blowing it back out.

There'd still been surprises at Thanksgiving. No matter how he'd tried to buffer her, tried to protect her and keep her from emotional hurt and pain, it had hunted and found her.

Road Runner and Aurelie had come. This was a couple Ester held a great fondness for, and she'd eagerly met them at the door. No shocks there, thank God. His patch brother Road Runner had looked startled when Ester had walked straight into his arms for a hug, but he'd smiled at her greeting, which would have been nonsensical to anyone but him. "Live free, and you do, and that's how I remember you best." She'd been referencing words the in-demand Chicago-based chef had tattooed on his knuckles, something Bones had heard her question him about a dozen times. Aurelie had been kind over the years the women had known each other, which earned her own welcome, a sideways hug that didn't last long, but Bones had known Aurelie understood what it cost Ester to offer even that.

His Ester was sweet and loving, but burdened by her past. Demons dogged her steps, flowing through her movements and words, causing her limbs to betray her at times, or her head. *I love her as she is.* The thought was accompanied by an emotion so fierce Bones' skin heated in response. *I love her.* There was no justification, no excusing, no downplaying how he felt. He simply loved her as she was. Because she was how she was. Beautiful, quirky and fae, and beloved.

Bones waited and watched as a bundled-up Ester made her way in from outside. She paused a moment on the mat to stamp her feet in a flurry of gestures, concentrated on knocking the snow off her boots. Each motion a concert, a symphony of Ester punctuated by the staccato cries of the birds outside, their voices echoing her childlike movements.

His Ester was unique, a treasure Bones cherished, holding tight to her with both hands. He'd loved her as long as he'd known her, from the first moment when she held out her hand, quoting a ridiculous line from a movie as she rescued him. For some, he knew her particular brand of unique would seem to lean more towards unbalanced, or disturbed, but Bones understood her and trusted she was as solidly sane as anyone else. His Ester just had a different way of interacting with the world.

Plowboy and his girlfriend had come to Thanksgiving dinner, too. Regrettably, their arrival was the beginning of things going awry.

It was still up in the air if Bones could get past that, because Plowboy was a favorite of Ester's.

Though a member of the club now, the man had been a prospect when she first met him. From that day forwards, Ester insisted on calling him Crowder, for reasons only she and Plowboy fully understood. Bones hadn't known the girlfriend had a daughter, a pretty little redhead about six years old. Ester's cry of delight at finding the trio waiting on the steps had been loud and heartfelt, and Bones had met Plowboy's gaze over her head, his brother's expression sad and apologetic. He knew. He knew the situation because all Bones' brothers knew, but Plowboy hadn't realized until that exact moment what he'd bought by bringing the child along.

Sweet and shy, the little girl hadn't wandered far from her mother at first, but Ester had been determined. She'd persistently worked at winning her over so that before long, the girl was hanging from Ester's back like a monkey, arms wrapped around Ester's neck, holding tightly.

Then had come Red and his old lady, along with their surprise accompaniment of four grandchildren. Bones shook his head at the memory of Ester's glance over her shoulder, the tribe of children gathered at her feet. Her expression had been equal parts pleasure and pain, the fragility of her balance shining from her eyes. Then she'd turned back and giggled happiness at the kids, holding out her hands in a promise of safekeeping.

Each arrival had given the house yet another cadre of children to add to the corps already trailing behind Ester.

She'd been driven to please them all. Ice cream, pie, cake, piggyback rides, reading books, adventures in the garden—activity after activity, each spiraling into the other until it was a blur. It hadn't taken long for Bones' brothers and their old ladies to notice how frantic she'd become, spinning from one activity to the next with hardly a breath between. Then had come the looks from them, pitying and sad. Ester had seen, a quick glance back snagging her tight as if caught in a net, and Bones' heart stopped in his chest when she turned motionless in the living room, staring at him, her eyes welling with tears. Wordless, without a sound, she'd escaped to their bedroom, and he'd followed her, leaving their guests to see themselves out.

Bones held a bath towel out as she pushed the door closed behind her, shutting out the biting cold wind. She accepted the fluffy cloth and ruffled it across her hair, then down her face and neck, her gorgeous smiling face peeking through the folds at him. "Did you see them?" Still in her galoshes, she twisted to look out the window at the birdhouses now covered in colorful avian visitors. "They were all whoosh and booosh, then the quiet standing on my head as if I were a statue." She looked back at him. "I had so much fun. Feathered friends are my favorites."

"Indeed." He bent over and lifted her foot, slipping the boot off and setting it aside before he moved to the next. "And you seem to be a favorite of theirs." Straightening, he cupped her cold-reddened cheeks in his palms. "You are chilled through, my Ester. Sit, and I will make cocoa."

She shivered and nodded, made her way to the table and jumped to sit on it, facing the garden. She could sit like that for hours, staring at the birds as they ate the feast spread before them. Birds, bunnies, stray cats and dogs, Ester adopted anything that looked to need mothering and care. She loved them all.

It wasn't that Ester didn't like kids.

She just couldn't have any of her own.

**

"What party?" Bones placed his fresh drink on the coffee table and then rolled his neck, wincing when it popped and cracked. "I was unaware of a mandatory party." He finished the stretching movement and leaned his head against the back of the couch. He glared over at Red. "I am certainly unaware of approving such. Are we expecting all members?"

"Yeah, that's what I heard from Tater." Red shrugged as he leaned sideways to pull a kerchief from his back pocket. He took his glasses off, using the soft fabric to buff the shiny surfaces. He lifted them to check his progress and scowled. "Dammit. I fuckin' hate these things. Jesus, gettin' old is a bitch."

"You feel yourself to be old?" Bones didn't bother to hide his shock. "You are younger than I am."

"Rode hard, brother." Red shook his head with a grin. "Been put up wet one too many times, I guess. Comes with the territory."

"You have children, yes?" Bones watched him slide the glasses back into place. "Two girls, if I remember correctly?"

"Hardly children anymore. My oldest is twenty next month, and her sister is only a year behind her." Red smiled broadly, eyes curved into commas with pleasure. "God willing, I won't be a grandpa for a long time yet, but I do love my girls."

"Can you imagine your life without them?" Bones didn't miss the flinch Red gave at his question. "I do not mean that in a coarse way, but my Ester…" He paused to take a deep breath. "You know the challenge, yes?"

"Yeah, brother." Red's voice was filled with pain, and Bones knew it was for him. "She wanted a kid, right?" Bones nodded, even if the tense wasn't right. *She wants one.* Red's voice lowered as he said, "I'm sorry, Bones. I wish I could do something. I'd do anything to help her."

"But there is nothing to be done. I know." He scrubbed across his chin, digging fingertips into the scruff along his cheeks. "Ester wants children. She cannot have them. These are facts in my life."

9

"Do you?" This came from behind him, and Bones arched his neck, looking over towards the bar to find the man associated with the familiar voice.

"Mason. I did not know you would be here today." He pushed to his feet and crossed the distance, wrapping an arm around the shoulders of his oldest friend. They exchanged back poundings, fists thumping vigorously, almost to the point of pain. "It is good to see you, my friend."

"Good to be seen, brother." Mason crooked a finger at the prospect behind the bar and walked to where Red stood, exchanging another warrior's embrace. "So"—he accepted the beer from the prospect with a nod—"do you?"

"Do I what?" Bones reclaimed his seat on the couch, elbows spread across the top of the cushions as he relaxed, knowing nothing could harm him here.

"Want kids?" Mason studied him as he asked the question, and Bones felt the heavy scrutiny like a weight on his skin. "You missin' having rug rats of your own?"

"I dream of seeing Ester's face on a child in my arms." He spoke plainly, with no inflection, doing his best to hold close and hide all the aching and hurt that single statement encompassed. "I watched my woman pull up every ounce of courage in her body to step foot inside a place that terrifies her, with good reason. My Ester willingly put herself into the maw of what she sees as a monster, to find answers. The doctors were gentle, they were kind, but the answers they gave us broke her inside.

Word by word, they broke parts from her soul and left them scattered at her feet. I prayed to the saints that it was my failure, so I could take it on myself to correct however that came about. It is not, and that slices deep, brother." He took in a deep breath, steadying his voice to continue.

"It is my mission to have her understand she is not less than, to see herself as I do, which is perfection. But when she cries at night, it is because her arms are empty, because she cannot hold a child created by the love we share, and that pain, that agony, it is not easily comforted. If I could, I would rip my heart free from my chest in payment for her dream. I would ply her with gifts to distract her mind, but you know my Ester. She wants doings, not things, and the doings she most desires are out of reach. It is not fair, this life, because she is the most gentle, understanding, loving, and loyal woman I know. Her protective streak runs broad and deep, and it well covers those helpless creatures that need it most. My Ester would make a fierce mother. She would be one who wouldn't shy from hard times, and would love a child more than breath."

Leaning forwards, he picked up his drink and downed it in three hard swallows, licking away the traces of whiskey that left smears on his lips. "So yes." He lifted his chin and stared at Mason. "My brother. I do want children with Ester."

"God damn," Red muttered thickly and turned away.

Mason held Bones' gaze for a long moment. Pain slid across his features and he leaned close, gripping Bones' shoulder in a tight grip. "If I can do anything to make that dream come true, all you have to do is speak it, and I'll break my back for you. Love you, brother."

"Love and respect, brother. I know you would." He pulled away and settled against the cushions again. "Now, tell me of this party."

Chapter Two
Bones

"My Ester, where are you?" He stood just inside the door and looked around in shock. "It looks as if there were a devil wind loose in our house." There were containers everywhere, stacked in tottering towers along the walls, electrical wires escaping in loops out of boxes, the shine of colored glass peeking through gaps where lids had been left askew. "A wild wind."

A lilting giggle drifted out from the room where his office was. "We're not in Kansas."

"No, we are not." He pushed the door open wide and stepped inside, stopping abruptly. "Ester." He stared at her. "What are we doing in our not-Kansas house of wind?"

"You're home early." Her tone was riding the edge of complaining, but he heard the smile there, too, and knew she wasn't truly cross. "How can I surprise you if you come home without warning?"

"Should I go away again, then?" As he'd expected, the threat of him leaving drove her from the shadows of the office and into the light, her head shaking violently back and forth, hair flying around her face. "You wish me to stay, little one?" A vehement nod set her hair adrift again, giving her the look of a partying head-banger. "Then I shall stay. If there is aught you want me to ignore, or avoid, to set your surprise in play, just tell me."

"The bedroom is safe." She peeked at him from behind a fall of hair. Shiny and clean, it stood in stark contrast from the first time he'd seen her. Still, even homeless and living on the street for more than a decade, she'd been as tidy as she could be, utilizing showers and laundry facilities where they could be found. Now, after years of good food, regular rest, and all the girly hair products she'd allow him to purchase for her, she was as gorgeous as the promise he'd seen behind the grime and fatigue.

"Then I shall wait for you in our bedroom." Even after so long, Ester still had trouble thinking of anything in their house as hers, including laying claim to something like a room. Bones liked to remind her as often as he could. "Will you be long, my Ester?" She smiled and shook her head gently. "May I have a kiss before I go up?" A quick nod answered his question, and she stepped over boxes to come to him.

Tilting her head back, she sighed softly as she offered him her lips. Her hands were behind her back, but when he covered her mouth, her entire body arched towards him, breast to chest, and belly to belly. Soft and giving, her lips molded to his and when he stroked his tongue along the seam of her mouth, she eagerly opened to him.

She tasted of cocoa, sugary sweetness, and longing. Carried up from a deep well inside her, the desire for him marked her. Long moments fled past as he kissed her thoroughly. Licking and sucking at her tongue and lips, he drew desperate sounds and half-formed words from her. He pulled back until their foreheads pressed together and then took a moment to breathe her in, smelling chocolate and peppermint, and arousal.

He smiled, touched his lips to hers a final time and promised her, "I'll always wait for you."

***

Ester

It was the sound of a dozen or more bikes that woke me. Rumbling into the room, the noises of engines and exhausts burrowed under the covers with me where I napped.

I'd been up early to watch the daily parade of pampered pooches, the group of them prowling at the ends of their leashes, dressed for their excursion in raincoats and tiny boots. Every morning, rain or shine, our neighbor gathered his pack and they became park-bound, from the tiniest Chihuahua named Dozer to the Great Dane I called Tiny.

Each dog knew me, and as I saw things, I knew they were as excited to see me as I was them. I'd placed one of them with the man, rescued and placed with someone my Bonesy had said once had more money than common sense, a saying I had enough sense of my own to not repeat. So, the dogs expected to see me, and greeted me, tails wagging and tongues lashing painlessly. Hellos and goodbyes mixed and blurred in passing until they were beyond me in many ways. The man had called out an invitation I'd been happy to oblige, absenting myself from Bones' house for sixty minutes only.

I'd been tired from the night before. It had been harder than I thought it would be, wrestling boxes in from the garage where Crowder had stored them for me. Bonesy had been out late communing with his brothers, and I took the rare opportunity to prepare for the wonderland I had planned. He most often was with me when darkness fell, which came earlier this time of year, the world drawing into itself and resting. Conserving energy for the burst of green growth springtime always brought. But my Bonesy had adapted easily, wordlessly, which was to say without me asking or him consenting, simply showing at the end of the day, no matter the time on the clock stated by fingerless hands pointing at meaningless numbers. By my reckoning, when the sun was up, it was time to work and be busy; if the sun was down, it was time for rest.

So, I'd been up late with wrestling of the two kinds, working and loving, the latter of which I confessed was my favorite of the two. Who wouldn't feel the same, given the chance to be loved by a man such as Bones?

But whoever wasn't the same were on their own, because he was all mine.

He's mine and I'm his.

I smoothed the frown from my brow, laughing at my fierce reaction to the thought of another's body under his hands. It was senseless to be distraught by such a thing that would never, could never happen. And my body under his hands *was* a memory to be worshipped, adored as I did him, holding close the moments where he gave himself to me. *I'm on his skin.* I took a moment to remind myself, my mind conjuring as if by magic a mental image of the me on him that he'd inked. No other woman shared that, except for his baby sister, lost in the shadows of death and time. I felt honored to be so paired with his Estrella, knowing how he'd loved her.

My mind settled for a moment and I arched my neck, remembering the feel of his colored canvas against my blank one. Skin tingling at the thought of the way his fingers traced the veins in my throat, the muscles of my arms, the curves of my stomach.

My hand dipped unbidden towards my flat belly, but I drew it up short.

No going there for me today, I promised, and settled my mind back to remembering. So, the wrestling had been followed by up early and playing, because I couldn't follow the dogs to the park and not play, could I? It had all conspired and combined to wear me out. Hence the napping.

I wasn't body sick, hadn't been for longer than I could remember. Back when I first found Bones, our friend Red's prescribed plan of nutrition, rest, vitamins, and generous application of love colluded with my body to buoy it up, plotting and succeeding at keeping sickness at bay. Okay, maybe he hadn't said anything about love, but being well had coordinated with loving Bones, so it felt to me that there was something to be said for the emotion. *Not quite enough of the truth*. I paused, considering said thought, and the corners of my mouth tipped skyward. Both the emotion *and* the action, because being body weary, worn from loving Bones always gave me the best sleeps in the history of ever. Yes, I decided with a nod. The action must be a critical application in the campaign of love against sickness.

What I was, was heartsick. Still recovering from a lifelong scarcity of never-enough, I found myself staring out into the look-ahead tunnel without seeing a rescue train coming my way. Heartsick and heartsore, and as much as I tried to tell myself it didn't matter, it did. Long ago days of pain and grief reached bony fingers into my today to twist it awry.

Every child I saw on the street was a blow to my bleeding heart. Happy was I, and I was when my Bonesy's friends celebrated their blessings. Still, my heart pumped poison in my chest, the beat echoing through my veins with a chorus of *not enough*. I would never be enough.

I had come to this wanting reluctantly, approaching it as a what-if and a maybe-someday only to find myself stuck at the corner of can't and never.

In the beginning, it was Bones and me, and that was all I needed. Then Mason's wife became my friend, and I'd held Willa's tiny human, losing my heart in different ways to the clutching of Dolly's tiny, perfect fists. That baby girl had changed my insides, and would always be my favorite in their house. Garrett did hold a close second, because of how protective he was. Like father, like son, and then I had wondered what a son for Bones would be like, and *oh*, the world could do with another dose of Bonesy.

That single moment of meeting Dolly had started the avalanche of thinkings and feelings, and then once I'd rounded the curve from not I, it felt like the straightaway would race me to the ending, because Bones had jumped on the running board of the right-now wagon with eyes shining the "God, yes please" look he only had for me.

Then came the weeks of waiting followed by scarlet drops of disappointment, followed by more hours of waning hope torn apart by the blood of my loins. Twelve losses, which was close to my luckiest number, but I didn't have much belief left in me at that point. Finally, he had broached the subject straight on, after a dozen sideways attempts I'd derailed, still looking for that rescue train.

Red had been my rock, and promised me safety if I talked to the white-coated demons. Those anti-angels I'd ceased trusting eons ago. I'd thought Red had sworn, mostly because Bones had vowed to finish him if he stepped wrong. I'd laughed at that, because they were brothers, and Bones would do anything for those he carried loyalty-love. In turn, Red laughed at me, coaching me in the greater importance of heart-love.

I allowed how he was right but wrong in the same breath, because brotherhood had made the high-water mark of Bones-love, giving me something to measure against.

Red agreed finally, but then *he'd* told me I erred in my assumptions as to the why he'd wanted to help in the first place, naming me his friend in a moment that struck me mute. Still, he knew what my silence meant; he'd ducked his head with a smile I'd seen him aim at his daughters. It warmed me from the inside out, and I loved him then. Loved him still, as a near-father, not that I remembered much about mine.

So Red had gone ahead of us, carving a path through claustrophobic hallways while Bones' arm wrapped tight around my shoulders. He curved around me as a safeguard, his body shielding mine against any dangers we might meet. For the perils in my head, he gave me his voice in my ear, scent in my nose, and love, always so much love in my heart for him.

He wasn't holding me back from leaving, but anchored me to him in a way that let me borrow his courage. Strong, warm muscles under my hands, hot blood in his veins, Ester-love in his steady gaze. Then it was gooseflesh, with the cold table under my bare bottom, cold fingers probing intimately, that personal touch frighteningly impersonal. It was only Bones' blazing eyes that gave me peace. In that love-forged calmness, I let my mind run free with memories of him as we'd come to know each other. Moment after blessed moment, my dark angel saving me all over again.

Red's voice murmured in the background, pitched to be ignorable and so I did. Bones' voice flowed through the air in his unique cadence, careful questions unanswered by audible words. There'd been quiet in the room finally, cold jelly wiped from my belly, and Bones had held me while I cried. It all meant there were no more reasons to wait, because the fallow fields of Ester would forever be barren. My body had missed the station, and there would never be a train for me.

My insides didn't match my outsides, and because of that, I didn't speak for a week.

But that was then, and this was now, and I'd come to terms with all the things it meant.

The roaring of bikes outside died away, final engine revs truncated by what I knew would be automatic switch flipping and easy leg swinging. I stared at the door, expecting it to blow open any moment, the return of my Bones imminent. I was not disappointed. He strode in with head high, eyes bright, smile wide and showing teeth. He was happy, proud, and excited, and I loved all of him.

Along with Bones came the close cadre of men he counted as his brothers.

Red and Shades, two men I trusted with Bones' life. Tater and Isabella followed them in, and then I was up and off the couch in a rush, my legs unsteady with the thundering force of my heart's emotion until my Ronnie's arms wrapped around me. I hadn't seen him in forever and a day, which if you counted as I did was an eternity too long. His Mouse was with him, an indulgent smile on the man's face at seeing my brother happy. Grinning and laughing from deep inside his middle, Myron didn't make me wonder at how he felt. He showed it to me right there, no guesswork, and I loved him a little more for always giving me that.

"I see where I stand in priorities." Bones' voice had dropped to a gravel-filled growl, much like the Great Dane's this morning in the park when asked to give up a favored toy.

I looked at him over Myron's shoulder, surprised to see an un-something on his face. Unhappy wasn't quite the word, but unpleasant wasn't even close. It was a not-something that bothered me, because when he looked at me, Bones most often shared a satisfied pleasure with the world. Ever afraid, my mind raced to find the cause, and I could only point fingers back at myself.

With a pat of Myron's shoulder, I pushed away, taking two steps towards the stairs. "I'm sorry." Throat so dry it ticked with those sounds I forced out, and they weren't enough. Couldn't be enough. So, I looked for another pair, aiming for politeness. Eyes aimed at the floor, I dodged away from Myron's reaching hands. "Good night, everyone." I couldn't stand the idea of the whole world seeing Bones upset, so removing the me part of the equation was the only solution I could figure.

"Ester." Two steps in and walking away wasn't yet easier. *Shouldn't it be easier?* "Ester, wait." Four treads in the past, dozens to go. "Baby." And that stuck my feet in their tracks. Bones always could do that to me. "Make yourselves at home; you know where everything is." That last was for his guests, and the words were a mimicry of what he told me often, in my mind lodging me in the same ranking as the men currently fanning out throughout Bones' house.

Heat from his body curled around me, warming my outsides in, and then his hands were on my arms. Palms to my skin, he slipped his hold down, grasping my wrists and pulling them in a crisscross, weaving our limbs like vines across the front of my body. Held thusly, I couldn't move, nor would I want to, since Bones was forever and ever my favorite place to be. Nothing else mattered about the where, just the who, and he needed to know that, so I gave it to him right away. "There's love enough inside me."

"I know, my Ester." His voice wisped through my hair, reaching my ears with a soft sigh. "I know you love me."

"It's not an emptied bucket." Not like the one I'd used for the bird baths this winter, filling it to the brim inside the house where the ice wasn't and hauled by muscle and might to the outside, where the warmth wasn't. "I won't spill it, Bones. I promise." Water scattered by my clumsy feet to splinter in icy shards against the ground. "It's artesian." The woman at the co-op had talked about that type of well, water free-flowing without a pump, sparkling liquid escaping the bonds of the earth with joy. "What's inside me."

"I know, baby." I stopped twisting my fingers into impotent circles, reaching for words I couldn't find in my head. When he called me baby, it was like a coveted comfort inside, where the word in his voice spread across the waves of discontent and anxiety, covering and smothering, but only in good ways. Only in ways that kept me from being lost inside my head until he couldn't find me. "Myron is excited to see you."

"Was." Like the stairs behind me, any pleasure in the night was a gone past thing. I'd broken that liking for him by bringing Bones' displeasure to his feet.

"*Is*, Ester. You were all he could talk about at the clubhouse. He couldn't wait to see you, and I expected the same from you. My words were an ill-chosen jest, and I wish I could call them back." His arms tightened around me, and I leaned against his chest, knowing he could hold me. My Bones could hold me up with one finger, but he liked more of me against more of him, so he'd always err on the side of all of him with me. "I know you love me. You show me every day with your doings."

"I'm not a stick." Tiny's darkly dappled face danced in my head, his broad brow wrinkled from arguing ownership with slobbering growls that held no heat. "I'm—" I stopped there, because my mouth stalled out on me, fearful lips holding fast to each other and trapping my words inside.

"You are mine." He rubbed his cheek against mine, and I smiled at how the scruff of his beard caught at my hair, wanting to hold onto it longer. His voice rolled and raged in quiet, the anger at himself swallowed until it was scarcely there, but I heard it. "You are mine, and I love you more than I can express. My words fail me, Ester."

"Mine, too." I piped that out like one of the birds waiting on seed, impatient to share their need. *He's my needing*. Quick and shrill my words, wanting him to know we shared sameness. "Can I…" I only allowed my throat a single pause to swallow the bitter back down. One and done, and then I asked permission from the part of my heart that lived outside my body. "Can I kiss you, Bones?"

"If ever you find yourself so inclined, there need be no askings, my Ester." His hold relaxed, and I twisted around in the powerful circle, not wanting to lose him entirely. He had his chin dipped to his neck and he looked at me with sweet longing. "Only doings."

So, I did him, right there on the stairs, with my brother and his brothers watching, not caring when Bones growled his tiny growl at their happy shouts.

***

Bones

Slowly, too slowly, Ester came back to life. With every second that ticked past and she still wasn't where she should have been with a house filled with their friends, Bones hated himself a little more. The joy on her face when she'd seen Myron had been worth anything, and if Bones had harbored a tiny slice of jealousy at how she loved her brother, he should have reminded himself of the previous night, or that morning, or any of a thousand moments Ester had given him to show she loved him, too. It didn't make sense to him, how that tiny bit of green had whipped free so quickly. Seeing the love of his life close down had torn him up inside, and he'd vowed to himself to keep a tighter rein.

She straddled the arm of the couch, hip by his head so he could look up at her face. Ester was focused on something Red was telling her, eyes wide in surprise. Bones watched her. She tilted her head and frowned suddenly, then burst into laughter, lips pulled wide in amusement at whatever story Red had spun. As if she could feel his gaze upon her, she glanced down at Bones, the laughter changing subtly to a pleased happiness.

She loves me. That was something he knew without a doubt. At some point in his life, he had done enough good for God to send him this angel. Bones lifted his chin slightly, and she didn't make him wait, swooping down to place her mouth over his in a firm press, lips dragging to the corner of his mouth where she dropped a quick kiss on the skin of his cheek.

Her name was called from across the room, and Bones watched Isabella smile at Ester. The woman had decided Ester needed to be her best friend, titling her nearly a year ago with no argument from Ester. He didn't think either of them had much experience with female friends—Ester from the isolation of being homeless for so long, and Bella because she'd been raised in a male-centric club in New Mexico. Her near-sister was Carmela, and those two girls were thick as thieves, but Mela had moved to California with her old man, Hurley.

Bella waved urgently, her hands making swirling motions in front of her that Bones didn't try to decipher. Ester seemed to understand, pushing off the couch to stand. She laughed sharply in surprise when Bones pulled her down to his lap. "Please, my Ester." Nuzzling against the side of her neck, he was rewarded by her hand on his head, fingers threading through and tightening on the hair he'd grown for that purpose.

"Whatever you need, Bones." Ester's whisper was quiet, words spoken softly next to his ear. "Any needing."

"One kiss, my heart." Lips to her cheek, he told her the truth. "I want more, I need more, but for now, a kiss will do." She melted against him, and he found her mouth with his, following a well-known dance of lips and tongue, letting her lead at times, then taking it back until she called his name, need coloring her voice with sweet promise. "Later, I will collect on the *any* portion." She shivered in his arms when he assured her that, and Bones smiled, setting her upright. Hands to her hips, he steadied her, then released his hold, knowing she would always return to him.

Head bent, she sat listening closely to Bella, and Bones breathed easier as Ester's profile slowly relaxed. The apple of her cheek lifted, a smile he couldn't see creasing her face, and he sighed. He had talked to Bella before the group left the clubhouse, hoping that the pain of the ask would be less coming from another woman. The club's party would be in three weeks, and he didn't know when he would pull together the courage to ask Ester to go. *Would that her life was always like this.*

Bringing in a houseful of his brothers and their friends had been a risk, but Myron's presence had made it easier to agree.

As if his thoughts conjured the man, Myron spoke from beside him.

"She looks good, brother."

Bones nodded, gaze still locked on Ester. She and Bella were holding hands now, Bella shaking Ester's back and forth in excitement. She glanced at him over her shoulder, caught him studying her and shook her head. Then she rolled her eyes before turning back to Bella, and Bones didn't try to stifle his laughter, knowing she heard him when she shook her head again, hair flying back and forth. *She will be with me.*

"She does." Drawing breath in on a sigh, he looked up to where Myron stood next to the couch. "It was a good call to have Mica watch your little girl tonight, though."

"Talya loves her Aunt Ester, but she also enjoys spending time with Jon and Tomas. It wasn't a hard sell."

Natalya was Myron's adopted daughter, shared with his husband, Andy. Jon was the son of Mica and Daniel Rupert, and Tomas belonged to Mica's sister, Molly, and her husband, J.J. Rupert, long time and valued friends of the club.

"It was kind of you to offer. I know Mouse does not like to be away from Talya often." Myron's grin was broad, and it was strong proof he was Ester's brother, because it showed the man's delight just as hers always did. "What?"

"Me and Andy booked into a room at the Admiral. Road got us upgraded to a suite. It's pretty nice. Quiet." He tipped his head to the side and waited. Bones shook his head, not understanding. "You know. Without kids?" Bones studied him for a moment, still puzzled as Myron's smiled stretched wider. "No Talya means it's daddy time."

"Oh, sweet Jesus in a basket." Red's muttered quietly from the other side of Myron. "Please, God, tell me you don't call him daddy." Myron's lips quirked, and his smile morphed into an evil grin. Red grunted like he'd been punched. "God, no. You can't do that shit, Myron. My old lady likes to call me daddy." His voice rose to a high quaver, and he called out in imitation, "Oh, Daddy. Spank me, Daddy." Voice returning to normal, Red said, "I do not need to have a visual of you bonin' Mouse the next time she's lookin' over her shoulder at me. Fuck you, Myron. You've ruined it for me now."

Bones tipped his head back and laughed hard. "You are both absurd."

He tensed when Ester took a step back from Bella, head shaking back and forth. She pulled her hands free, and he watched as her fists clenched, then unclenched, arms stiff at her sides. Bella leaned closer, the expression on her face earnest, and just as Bones was ready to push off the couch, Ester nodded once. She bent towards Bella, and he watched in surprise as she rested her cheek on Bella's shoulder for a moment. The smile on Bella's face was blinding, and she recovered quickly, wrapping Ester in her arms, holding her close.

"It's gonna be okay." Bones looked up to see Myron's eyes were locked on Ester, too. "You're strong enough for both of you when you need to be, Bones. She'll struggle. Maybe for a while, but you'll figure it out, and then together you'll move forwards."

A hand landed on his shoulder and he heard Shades' familiar voice. "You know how you always say she makes you a better man?" Bones nodded, unable to speak at the way his brothers were circling around him protectively. "Well, you make her a better woman, too. Ester's strong, and she's it for you, brother. Blind man could see it. And me? I'm not blind, which means I see you're it for her, too. You'll get through this, Bones. It's a rough patch, no doubt, but you'll get through it."

Bones started to answer just as the phone in the study rang once. He listened closely, heard murmuring voices and nodded. One of the men in there had answered. Probably club business, which meant he'd have to get up anyway, so he pushed off the couch and stood. Plowboy walked to the door and stared out, sweeping the crowd with his gaze. "Ester, the phone is for you."

She froze in place and turned to stare at Bones with wide eyes. He nodded encouragingly and touched a fingertip to his chest in a silent question. Her bobbing head was answer enough, so Bones followed her as she made her way to the study. Once inside, he took the cordless device from Plowboy with a muttered,

"Thanks," and went directly to the desk, punching the button to put the call on speaker. "Ester can hear you." She wouldn't talk on the phone yet, not unless he forced her, and after thrusting an impromptu party upon her, there was no way he would do that to her now. She drifted in close behind him, placed her palms on his waist, her fingers twisted tight in the belt loops of his pants. There was silence, so he prompted, "What do you need?"

"Ester's there?" It was a man's voice, and Bones' jealousy stirred again, teeth grinding tight together. "She's on the call?"

"Yes. As I said, she can hear you." He swallowed hard, muscles of his jaw burning with the drive to hurt something, hurt someone, *this* someone specifically because the man thought nothing of holding her name in his mouth. *She's mine.* "What do you want?"

"Tell her Goliath isn't working out." Bones startled when Ester's head popped around his shoulder, her eyes narrowed as she glared at the phone. "She needs to figure something else for him."

"Goliath?" Bones was confused by the name. This was no one he'd heard about from Ester before, and definitely wasn't a club member. He would have remembered a name such as that, threaded through with dominance. "Who is that?"

"Tiny." Quiet, the single word shook, and Bones wrapped an arm around Ester's shoulders. She moved more fully in front of him, head angled down to look at the phone. "His name is Tiny."

"Doesn't matter what he's called, Ester." The man's tone had changed, turned arrogant in a way he hadn't sounded when speaking to Bones, and that very change angered Bones more. Through the speaker, he heard barking and finally realized this had to be about one of her rescues. "He isn't a fit for me. You need to come get him." A pause, then louder, an attempt to command without realizing he was speaking to a room full of men far more dominant than whoever this was on the phone could ever be. "Come get him now."

"His name is Tiny." Her frame shook as badly as her voice, and it took Bones a moment to realize this was anger driving his woman. "Not Goliath."

***

Ester

Eric Nettic had called Bones' house. He wasn't supposed to; the rules for fostering and adoption were clear. Calls were to be directed to the center only. But because he knew me, or thought he did, this man had somehow found it inside him to call here, putting himself smack within the walls of my sanctuary. I hated him a little right then, but I couldn't focus on the me-anger, because I could hear the barking and whimpering in the silences between his words. So I let the Tiny-anger take over, carrying me through the breaking wave that let me harness it and speak.

"His name is Tiny." It was, too, no matter what Eric not-nice Nettic called the Great Dane. "Not Goliath." Bones pulled me sideways so my shoulder hit his ribs, his arm tight around my shoulder. I needed that hold right then to keep me from launching myself through the phone to strangle the man who'd made my brave dog sound like that.

"Goliath," he hissed, stubborn to a fault. I should have known better. "But like I said, it doesn't matter what his name is, you need to come get the dog now. I think it's because you insisted on having him fixed. He's cowing down to my Dozer, Ester. I can't have him here like this."

"Taking that tone with my woman is not wise, asshole. Watch yourself." Bones was vibrating in place, muscles clenching in his arms. I spoke over him, wanting to make my point clear, because Eric not-nice Nettic was wrong about the dog.

"He can't be what his name is as long as you call him Goliath, no matter what you want. Wantings don't get you what you need, and you only think you need what you have. That dog will never be a Goliath, because in his heart he's Tiny. Your mind wants a dog that can be a Goliath, but you...that's not what you *need*. Because a Goliath would fight you, argue with you, tell you you're wrong, and you'd have to convince them you know best."

I tried breathing through my nose to calm down, a trick the yoga instructor at the co-op had shared.

It didn't work.

"Goliaths aren't pets, they're partners, and that is *not, not, not* what you need, Eric. Mister not-nice Nettic. Your heart needs a Tiny. A dog that's willing to take what you give, and they love you for the least of your attention, because that's all you'll ever have to give them."

Bones was looking me with the oddest expression on his face. Shock warring for space with pride, but I couldn't give that any space in my head right now.

This man, this Eric Nettic, had riled me up. I was a pup momma right now, and I let the bitch take me where she needed to go. The anger buoyed me up, lifted me to my toes as I shouted towards the phone, willing Tiny to hear me and know I was coming. I was coming right *now*. I wrinkled my lip up and stuck my tongue out at the phone. *He's not a good dog daddy.*

"He deserves more than that. He deserves everything. He deserves to be trusted to know what he needs to be. You want to think you're bigger than you are, so you try to force the Tiny dog into the role you carved out for him. But you don't stop to wonder if he's happy there, or if he was happier where he was. Well, you can bet your bippy butt I'll be coming to get him. I'll be there in five minutes, Eric not-nice Nettic. And if you call him Goliath one. More. Time." I hesitated, then decided if the ferocity inside me was a momma dog fighting for her pup, then I wouldn't worry about nice. "I'll kick you so hard you'll wish the vet would have fixed you instead."

I reached out and rapped my fist against the glowing button on the box, then backed away, putting Bones between it and me. He didn't move, and I was glad, because I could only adjust to one overwhelming change in the room at once. And me talking to Eric not-nice Nettic on the phone was big.

"I'm glad that wasn't video." The couple of times I'd chatted with Myron through Bones' phone, he'd held it across the room, letting me see my brother's face from afar but still close enough to watch him smile. "I need to go get a dog."

Bones asked, "Will the center be open?" I tugged on one side of Bones' jeans and he turned to face me. I shook my head. His eyes drew a zigzag line across my features, nostrils flaring. He brought his hands up to cup the back of my neck. "Ester, what will you do with the dog?"

I didn't think, didn't care, only knew I had to go, and these questions were holding me back from doing what Tiny needed. What I needed. Momma needed to rescue her pup. "Tiny can come here."

Bones looked alarmed. For all he knew, I loved dogs. He'd only asked once or twice, and then things had gotten crazy, and then I'd gone crazy again, and I hadn't brought it up again. He stared at me and stared at me, and then his shoulders lowered, expression softening. "Okay."

"I'll go with her." Myron's voice was right behind me, and Bones' gaze flicked up and back down. I nodded.

He should stay. But I *had* to go, and he recognized both of those in a moment.

"Where does this man live? He was not kind when he spoke to you, my Ester." Gaze back up over my shoulder, and I knew his next words were for Myron. "You do not allow that in person."

"No, brother. You know I've got her." Myron's hand was solid and warm when he dropped it at the back of my neck, fingers and thumb giving me a squeeze that made my whole chest warm.

"I have to go."

Bones' gaze dipped to my mouth, and I couldn't help it. Amid all my fury and rage at a man who didn't understand the beauty inside the dog entrusted to him, I melted a little when my man asked for a kiss. In his own way, using the language we held between us, he showed me. Myron's heat fell away when I leaned forwards, my hands propped on Bones' chest as I lifted to my toes. Carried there not by rage and anger this time, but by love.

Slowly, as if we were alone and had the whole of the night in front of us, I pressed my lips to his and he turned into a mirror, giving me an exact replica of love back. I kissed him and kissed him, and stored up that love inside my belly, lining my chest with it, holding it in every corner of my mind, ready in case I needed to bring it out and look at it. He bit at my bottom lip, gripping it gently with his teeth as he drifted away slightly. "I love you," I told him. It came out garbled without the use of both my lips, but I laughed at the look on his face. "You think I'm cute," I reminded him, and he nodded, taking my head with him, my lip still trapped in his teeth. "Bones, I gotta go." That earned my release because he needed to laugh, and he couldn't do it properly without his mouth on mine.

After he gave me laughing kisses, he backed away and looked over my shoulder again. "Bring her back safely."

We were out on the sidewalk and I'd turned towards Nettic's house without pause before Myron spoke. "So we're walkin'?" I nodded, pushing my legs to longer strides, wanting to eat up the blocks between me and where Tiny was. Myron's shadow stretched ahead of us for the moment, drawn there by the angle of the lights across the street. It looked as if his darkness was checking the cracks, ensuring our safety. I liked the idea of something innately my Ronnie worrying about me like that. "You like this dog, huh?"

I gave him a glance to see he wasn't joking like I thought. "Duh. It's a dog."

"Dogs and babies." His shadow nodded. I focused on that movement, willing him not to chase the topic further. I didn't get my wish, which was why they weren't any better than wantings. "How are you doin', Sissy? Bones seems happy."

"Seems?" I latched on that questioning word, because seeming and being were as far apart as the poles were on a globe of the earth. "He's not happy?" I needed

37

him happy, because without him, I wasn't the me I wanted to be. "Why? Did he say something?"

"No, honey. Not at all. What I meant to say is Bones is happy. Like you. You're happy, too. Right?" How could he state and ask all in the same sentence?

"Happier than Tiny is." I planted my toe and made a sharp turn up the walk towards Nettic MacNotNice's house. Myron overshot the walkway by a stride, but he ignored the precise lines of edged grass dividing walking spaces from not, his boots making crushed marks on the lawn.

I stopped and stared at the black that would be green in the daylight. Grass, from wall to walk, and on to the drive. Grass everywhere, and not a single yellowed spot of claiming by a dog. Not a toy, not a stick, not a solitary indication the man had a pack inside this not-a-home house.

"Packs claim, you know?" Myron made the humming noise he did when he didn't understand the shortcuts my brain made. "Like the club. You claim, and people know." I turned and gestured towards the street, lined on both sides by motorcycles. "Anyone driving past knows you're here, that you belong, that this place was made to welcome you." Bones' home had always been so, since the first time I woke in his bed. "The people claim, too. I'm Bones', and he doesn't hesitate to tell anyone, to show anyone. He pisses all over his property." I shook my head at Myron's hissing inrush of breath. "Not like that. No icky stuff. But if we're in a group, I'm steady because he's got me. Always. His hands, his side, his lips, his lap—no one wonders who I belong to, because he's proud to have me. Proud that I own him back. Proud that I carry him on my back." Receiving the "property of" vest had been a celebration in the club, and I loved wearing the heavy black extension of Bones' love. I thrust my thumb over my shoulder at the yard of Nettic's house. "This *man*," the word came out garbled, nearly growled, "has dogs, but you'd never know because he values things more than beings. Tiny doesn't belong here." I shook my head. "No dog belongs here."

"Ester." Myron's voice was low and aimed at calming, but I was about two giant mother-may-I strides beyond where that would work on me. "We're here for one dog."

"Tonight," I agreed, because I'd already decided to talk to the rescue president tomorrow morning as soon I could get Bones to agree to be my voice.

The door opened at the top of the short stack of steps, and Nettic stood there. I didn't give him the energy to name him, holding that back because the words I wanted to give him weren't his to hold. I saw the weaving head of my friend behind him and waved, angling my gaze to the side, measuring. Just enough room. Dropping to one knee, I held out my arms and called. "Tiny, come to Momma." The Dane wedged himself past Nettic's hip, gaining momentum as his gangling legs came to agreement with what his head and heart both wanted, and then he was out the door and onto the walk, barreling down towards me.

Myron's muttered "Fucking hell" from behind me didn't count as a greeting, so I decided to do introductions later. First chore to tackle was getting Tiny safe, and making sure he knew he would always be thus.

"Come here, come here, come here." Happy to comply, Tiny tucked his head at the last moment, slipping his muzzle and neck under my arm along my side, body curling around my front so his bony tail whipped at my back on the other side. "That's my good friend, my boy, my sweetie. You're safe, safe, safe. Always and forever safe." Trembling and whining, Tiny hugged me as best he could while I crooned a love song to him, chin resting on his spine.

***

Bones

Myron chuckled as Bones stared into the study. Ester had laid claim to the room, dispatching Plowboy to gather blankets so she could build a nest. "The look on your face, brother." Myron laughed again. "Priceless."

"That is not a dog. That is a horse." He should have known. He entirely understood the need of the dog's owner to rename the beast, because from nose to tail the monster spanned the length of the couch upon which he now stood. Head barely lifted over the back, Bones saw how the dog's dark eyes darted back and forth, first to Ester and then back to Bones. *Goliath indeed*. "What did the man say when you arrived?"

"Not a word." Myron chuckled. "We were on the front walk, and she was ranting about claiming and pissing, and then he opened the door, and she was like, 'Come to Momma.' Swear to God, her words, not mine. Dog nearly took the asshole down trying to get around him and down to where Ester knelt on the cement. Whole way back, he was pressed tight to her leg. No leash or anything, and he stayed with her stride for stride."

"Do you think the beast is safe?" Bones wished for Gunny; his advice would be valuable in this regard. But it was late, and even later in Fort Wayne. *I'll call him tomorrow*, he vowed. "She's so small next to him."

"You ever had a dog?"

Bones shook his head. "Closest I ever came was when I was a child. I walked my neighbor's dog."

"Well, I've had lots of experience with dogs, helping Gunny and PBJ. Trust me when I say *that* dog is no danger to Ester." Myron laughed softly. "Can't say the same for anyone who might want to hurt Ester, though. Watch this." Bones eyed the dog as Myron took a step into the room, watching as the head rose higher over the back of the couch. Another step, this towards Ester, earned a lifted lip, white fangs shining in the lights. "You watchin', brother?" Myron didn't take his gaze off the dog as he took a quick stride towards Ester, pulling to a stop when the room filled with a deep, dark growl, echoing off the walls until it had grown to a wild reverberation.

"Stop it, Tiny." At Ester's mild command, the dog's ears came back up from where they'd plastered against his skull and he quietened, lip again covering his sharp teeth. She didn't look up from what she was doing to the pile of blankets. "And that was mean, my Ronnie. Tiny's not small in courage; he just needs someone to drive. Like I need Bones for...everything. Tiny's not sure of you yet. Be nice."

She stood and stared down, hands propped on each hip, head angled so the line of her neck was exposed, and Bones felt an overwhelming need to kiss her just there. He took a step towards her and the dog's head lifted again, dark eyes fixed on him. "Hush, Tiny," he said, not ungently, and earned a smile over Ester's shoulder when the dog remained quiet as he made his way to where she stood. "My love, have you finished with the horse's bed?" He gave himself one kiss along the back of her neck and then leaned over her back, head beside hers as he looked down. There were three blankets twisted and twined in such a way they wouldn't separate even if the dog rolled in his sleep. There was a pair of Ester's socks, tied in the middle, pink unicorns bright on the dark fabric. And there was a stick, one that already had deep toothmarks dug into the wood, even though he hadn't seen the dog near where Ester had been working.

"He's a dog." She reassured him with a chuckle and then whistled brightly. The floor shook as Tiny's paws came off the couch, padding their direction. "Not a horse." The beast rubbed his side along Ester and Bones' thighs, managing to touch them with what felt like every inch of his body. "He's a good boy." She caressed the dog's head, then cupped his jaw and tipped it so Bones could see himself reflected in Tiny's eyes. He towered over Ester, and even more so over the dog, massive as Tiny seemed. "Tiny, this is Bones." Vertebra wrapped in thin skin rapped against the floor as the dog promptly sat on his haunches, tail blurring back and forth. "He's mine." She grabbed Bones' hand and brought it up to just under her breasts, pressing it against her flesh. "Be nice." She released the dog and pushed with her shoulders until Bones took a single step back, their feet now free from the entangling blankets. "Tiny, down." The floor shook again as the dog's elbows smacked hard, even through the cushioning she'd provided. "Stay." A thin keening sound filled the air, and the dog's head dipped closer to the floor. "Hush, you're fine. You're home, Tiny." The sound ceased, and Bones saw the dog's eyebrows tick up, eyes flicking back and forth from him to Ester and back again. "He'll love you, too." Another quick whine, and then the dog rested his head on the blankets, curling around to give them his back. "Jerk. You already love him." One solid thump of his tail and then Tiny sighed without moving, the sound going on and on until Bones realized that wasn't what was going on.

"Oh God," he gagged out, wafting his hand in front of his face.

"MacNotNice fed him bad food. It's not Tiny's fault." Ester didn't seem bothered by the stench, something Bones couldn't imagine. "It'll get better." She glanced up at him, a flicker of worry crossing her face. "It won't go away. But it will be better."

"You want to keep him." Not a question, because Ester had already laid claim. Bones had never seen her as fierce as she'd been on the phone, dressing down some man because he'd called to surrender this beast. She'd held her own with him, eloquent and clear, leaving no guesses as to how she felt about the man. If Ester wanted this dog, and this dog brought out that kind of fire in his woman, Bones would never naysay her. "I hope you do." He opened that door a little, giving her room to ask for what she wanted. What she needed.

"His needing is me." She shrugged, the motion jerky as if her muscles tried to block it. Head down, she played with Bones' fingers, keeping them pressed high on her stomach. "I can't say no to needings."

"And neither shall I. Welcome to our home, Tiny." *Thump.* The dog acknowledged Bones' use of his name, ears perking slightly.

Chapter Three
Ester

"Nyeaaat." I shook my head at Tiny just before he dipped his nose into the bucketful of warm water. It wasn't that I was denying him access to water, but the silly pup would freeze his lips off when we went outside. "Come on." I shrugged into my jacket and zipped it up before I opened the door, already shivering.

There had been a bitter turn in the weather the past two days, and I stepped in front of him with a shuffle, carefully breaking through the ice crust on the snow so he didn't bleed a pad. The air felt soft, cold but expectant, like it couldn't wait for the next layer of white to be laid down.

Already I could hear the rustling of wings and feathers as my friends crowded closer, ready to pounce on the water. In this kind of weather, water was harder to come by than a good feed, and I knew it well. The bone-deep chills caused from pulling body heat to melt even a mouthful of snow weren't something easily forgot. Tiny bumped me from behind, jostling the bucket with his head, trying to angle around the side. He wanted to get his zoomies on, muscles twitching with excitement. I stopped and stepped to my right, protecting the bucket as I gave him a clear path towards the back of the yard. "I can't save you from yourself," I reminded him. He wouldn't wear the booties Bones had bought him, used the edges of his front teeth to tease them off his toes, which meant he'd be barefooted on the ice and snow.

Bones. I shook my head. That had been a surprise. He'd bonded with Tiny quickly, starting from that first night. Bones had slept restlessly, and I'd woken the next morning to him already out of bed and dressed, muttering about some old lady who'd fed her dog better than she ate, and how Tiny had deserved better than MacNotNice. My name for the turd button, not his.

An hour later, Kevin showed up at Bones' home, coming inside with a knock and a yell, like he always did when he was Road Runner. Tiny roared his roar at him, and Kevin quickly dominated, making Tiny feel safe enough to lie by me. Bones had been on the phone, asking questions, and his ignoring for the call had driven Kevin to resorting to come and talk to me. What I didn't know until later was Bones had been calling the owner of a pet store nearby, having gotten his number from Ronnie, and dialed the man out of bed. Kevin, as Road Runner, had driven with Bones to the store that morning, coming back with a mass of things Bones determined were necessary to be a good pup dad.

So now Tiny's toots were less blistering, and he was the proud owner of two gigantic beds, a raised food and water dish, and enough toys to keep an entire pack amused.

I stopped and watched as the gangling dog, well past puppyhood, dashed out and across the hard surface of the snow. He was hilarious, trying to play as if he didn't weigh as much as a moose. With the enormous mass of his body stopping about as well as a car without brakes, I watched while his rear end actively slid out from under him. I laughed hard when he went chest-down to the ice, spinning in a slow circle as he slipped downhill, the shock on his face comical. "Ridiculous looks good on you, Tiny."

Moving slowly, giving him time to recover from his embarrassment and collect his splayed legs, I watered in the shallow bowls I'd brought out for this. It was so cold there was only one brave bird that attempted a bath, giving up quickly and hopping his way to the edge, sitting there looking miserable and wet, shivering violently. "Silly," I murmured and picked him up, putting him inside my jacket to let him warm up. Feed was next, and the flock followed me closely, making swiping runs at the seed that dribbled out of my dipper.

Bones had asked me that first fall why I stopped feeding the birds at the end of summer. For those summertime birds, it could be a matter of life or death, easy food tempting them to stay until the winter window closed on migration. He'd understood that well enough, but then called me to task when I resumed feeding just before Thanksgiving, a few days after the first real snow hit.

"People are fickle," I muttered. When it was cold out, it became harder to find filled feeders, or fresh, unfrozen water.

Those who'd tempted the flying beauties that surrounded me now had lost faith, their efforts abandoned for the warmth of their own homes. These birds would struggle, and many wouldn't see the spring, but if I fed them, then a few more would make it through. Stronger, smarter, and a better addition to the gene pool.

A gray nose popped into view, sniffing at the seed. Tiny jerked back when a small titmouse pecked at him, then came back, snuffling again. I stifled a laugh when the bird hopped on top of his head, balancing against the bend of one enormous ear. Tiny's eyes were big and round, rolled up in his head as if he could see through the roof of his mind. I snorted at the absurd look he wore. Surprise and worry, and a little bit of pleased. "You made a friend." It reminded me of Crowder's original attempts, hands out, mouth wide when the first tiny claws wrapped around his fingers. He'd been the same as Tiny, and I'd loved him for it. "You're a goof."

I reached out and gathered the bird in my hand, cradling him to my face for a quick ruffled feather touch. A stirring near my chest reminded me, and I brought out the now-dry and warm daredevil, setting both on the platform of a feeder. "Be good." They ignored my admonishment, immediately arguing about something. I shook my head.

Back inside, Tiny waited patiently for me to wipe his feet, and didn't even whine when I inspected to be certain his paws didn't harbor any scrapes from playtime. Once I was done, though, he was off. Head and tail up, feet pounding the floor in an urgent rhythm, he aimed arrow straight for the study where Bones was with Shades. I waited, listening, because unless they had locked the door, they were about to be interrupted.

Tiny pawed at the door twice, and when no one immediately opened it for him, he nosed the doorknob. I heard teeth on metal, and then a clinking crunch as he fitted his mouth to the grooves he'd already bent into the knob, twisting his whole head to get at his man. Pain gouged through my throat, closing all the air in my lungs for a moment. His daddy.

It was like a sickness how the aching came on me sometimes.

I'd believe myself past the worst of it, like the fever or weakness from the flu, and then I'd round a corner and the knowledge would smack me down. I'd been on my knees for weeks, months, thirteen of one and three of the other. "He'd be the best." Bones was made to be a father. Patient and loving with me, no matter how inside myself I folded. I'd seen it with the kids around the club, too. He looked at them with such longing at times, and then his gaze would come to me and land with a hollow thud, like I'd sucked all his dreams out of his heart.

I wanted to give him a tiny human. A being outside myself that he would love. Broken and useless inside, all I could grant were holes. Holes in his life where he could have been with someone else. Saying that was not smart, though. And I liked to think I'd gotten a slight bit smarter over the time I'd known him. Saying that to Bones had earned me somber lectures, brooding looks, and wounded sounds as he tried to reassure me. I knew. In my heart inside my chest, I knew he loved me. Loved *me*, not some made-up woman who wouldn't be broken. He loved me, and together we fit in a way no one else could.

We just couldn't fill in the rest of the breaks, because there'd be no tiny human for me.

So I'd worked hard and shoveled other things into the holes, fast as I could. If he didn't see how it hurt me, then he settled, and I liked Bones settled. He had enough in his life to worry about without me adding even more to that. I tackled the shelter's rescue dogs, making sure to let him see the true joy it handed me. Dogs in and out of the kennel at the rescue—most were breeds hard to place, and I was good at matching them with people. I set aside the disaster of Tiny and MacNotNicerson, since I figured Tiny was always meant to be here with us. With me. With Bones.

Bones' club helped, too. The kids. Oh, the kids. They were the best part of a family party, because they ran and played. Those wee ones were held in such care, they knew to the soles of their feet nothing could happen to them. Always watched and cared for, they were safer than the safest, surrounded by nothing but love.

Through the weeks and days I'd been finding ways to fill in the holes, but some days it was like sand in a sieve, trickling and tricking, until all my raw spots were back on display. It never stopped the pain for long.

Bones did. He could stop the pain with a word, with a look, with a touch, and I loved how he knew what I needed. Even without me telling him, he would know. "He's my joy." My dark angel, my savior who sexed me up on the regular. That helped more than anything, how he never let the broken pieces of me dictate his dick. We came together with laughter and love, and always I could count on him to bend me back into straight lines of love.

I loved my Ronnie, too. Of course I did. I couldn't just get him back and then not love him. But he had found Mouse, and I loved Mouse, too. And they had a little girl. Talya. I was her favorite aunt, and she wasn't shy about telling me. I didn't tell her it counted less since I was her only, because it didn't. She was earnest and beautiful, and sweet caramel goodness inside and out.

I heard a soft click from the study and knew it was Bones closing the door behind Tiny's self-invited entrance. I smiled and sighed, then went to the freezer. Pulling out the always-present container of ice cream, I dished up a bowl and took it and myself to the table.

He hadn't shut me out. Bones would never do that to me. I smiled again, looking out the window at the birds still arguing and talking about the goodness they'd been given today.

One foot on the chair, and one swinging in the breeze, I ate my ice cream slowly. A sweet spoonful at a time.

He'd shut himself in.

Not to keep himself from myself, but to keep the darkness of whatever he and Shades had to discuss from tainting the rest of the house. Always those conversations happened in his study. His office. The place where the club existed most strongly inside these walls.

I wasn't forbidden to go in there. Not at all. If business-free, I was welcomed there as in every room. He hadn't even complained when I'd finished setting up the wonderland for him. Today was his first chance to see the full glory, and he'd laughed mightily when I opened the doors. Then he'd flicked the switch that started the train on its looping path around the floor.

"Ester, the monster will destroy your creation." He shook his head even as his hands reached for my hips, pulling me close, belly to belly. "It is gorgeous."

I'd closed one eye, squinting with the other, preparing for the rejection I was sure was coming. When he stopped speaking, I opened both eyes wide, staring up at him. His gaze was so warm, so loving, I could nearly feel it like a touch as he stroked it across my skin. "You hate it less than I expected."

"I do not hate it at all." He bent his neck, and then it was his lips stroking a caress on mine, and that I could definitely feel. "I love it, my Ester." Tiny picked this

moment to mosey inside, pausing only a moment when Bones called his name. "Tiny, no." Ignoring the uncertain command, Tiny lifted his feet high and stepped across the train tracks, avoiding the glitter-infused cotton I'd used to create the snowfields. "He..." Bones shook his head as Tiny lurched up on the love seat, turning in place twice, so big he nearly fell off the cushions before he threw himself to his side with a groan that lifted his ribs high. "He is not like anything I expected."

"You expected a bad dog?" At those two words in close proximity, I saw Tiny's ears twitch. "He's a good dog."

Bones grinned at the single thump of a tail that greeted my words. "He is a good dog." Bones reached up and cupped a hand to the corner of my jaw. "And you are a good woman." The pain twitched inside me, just like Tiny's skin would if I were to tickle him with a feather. "Thank you for my wonderland. I've never had a Christmas like this."

He'd never had Christmas. Not since he was small, since before the day he died and came back, leaving Estrella on the other side of the veil. Our first Christmas had been a season of crazy days filled with club business, and no celebrating to be found. The second featured family additions in the form of Mouse. This was our year, and I'd determined to make memories here in Bones' house that he was so adamant be mine, too. I'd owned my place by stuffing the space full of things for him. "I wanted to give this to you." I gestured at the room, knowing he'd understand. "It's good to share firsts." I *hadn't been lucky with Christmases either, with most of them spent hoping I didn't freeze to death before the sun rose on just another day. I didn't say that, though. I'd learned what would make him mad or sad by turns. "I'm learning you."* He smiled, a one-sided lift of his mouth that promised so much. *"It's for both. You..."* I placed my palm over his heart, feeling it beating strongly under my touch. *"And me."* My lips ached for his, and he must have seen it in my eyes, because he bent down and gave me what I needed. Needings. *"I love you."* Straight out, because he always deserved to know.

"And I you, my Ester." Another kiss, this followed by his hand on my neck, and then down my arm, and then cupping the softness of my breast in his fingers. Clever fingers, teasing and using the sign language only he knew to draw my wordless response.

There was a tapping at the window, and I looked down to see Tiny's titmouse balanced on the edge, smallest of talons digging into the wood as it held on tightly. "He's in there." I gestured over my shoulder at the study. "He can come back out tomorrow." The bird tilted its head as if to see me better, then tapped impatiently on the window again. "Sorry, not tonight." Silly bird, asking for a playdate in the snow. Asking for doings.

I shoved another spoonful of cold, creamy goodness into my mouth and let it sit on my tongue, melting.

Doings were easier than things. Bones appreciated both, which made my living easier than it could have been. The wonderland was a things thing, and he hadn't hated it. I had money now, which was so weird to ponder, having been penny-poor for so long. The rescue valued what I did with them, and even though I'd have done it for free, just to be the helping part of the dogs' lives, they paid me a set amount every week. I wrinkled my nose at the titmouse still on the ledge. *Persistent fella.*

Gunny was persistent, too. He was the one who set up the rescue work for me. He had too much going on now with pups and tiny humans of his own.

My reflection in the windows was smiling so wide, I stared at me for a moment. Gunny's life was good. He and me, we'd talked once, about the coulda, woulda, shoulda, pieces of our past. He counted himself lucky to have found the club when he did. Inside his head had been messed up. He'd been like me, where he could blink and a day would be gone, or a week, and he'd have no remembering of any doings that he'd done. First the club, but even that hadn't been enough to steady him entirely. Still, the club got him ready for the bigger things that were coming. He didn't know it at the time, but his Sharon would fix him for always. Like Bones had me. Then his Sharon turned around and made his outside heart even larger. Cade, Kitten, and Josh. He'd said his family—including the pups, of course—were his reason for breathing. His reason for keeping his head straight and his mind strong.

"I want a child." There. I'd said it. Even if just to the tiny titmouse still watching through the window.

I cradled the bowl of ice cream goodness to my chest. Bones had wanted to talk about other ways, but I'd shut him down. Shut down myself and walked away.

I'd walked outside and dug in the wild garden until my fingers bled, forgetting the tiny shovel he'd bought me. I'd stayed outside for two days, waking on that last morning to find he'd slept beside me in the grass, covering us both with blankets from his bed. He never told me I was crazy. Had never once said those words that would tear me down. Never told me I didn't understand. He'd never tried to pretend he was anything except devastated at the way my body had betrayed me. Betrayed us both. But he'd also never blamed me. "He wants a child." *Tap, tap, tap.* Tiny's titmouse was staring at me.

Bones didn't care if it was a child of my body. That was a things. The biggest of things, but a things. It wasn't about the *having* a tiny human that mattered to him. It was about all the havings after. "It's the doings." My reflection was crying now, and I ate another bite of ice cream that tasted salty and sweet. *That's what he wants with me.* My voice was small but strong as I told the bird, "He wants the biggest doings in the history of ever with me."

And I'd shut him down.

"He wanted to live." With me. Wanted me to take that journey with him any way we could go. He'd shoved his hand out at me again and again, waiting for me to take hold. "Wanted to save me." Bones already had saved me. Time and over and gone, he'd saved me. Every day when I woke up with his body beside me, his hand in my hair, his leg cocked over my ass, and his cock legging its own way up my hip, he saved me. My dark angel.

"Found treasures are important, too." I remembered a scarf I'd had for years. It had been tattered and dirty when I found it, but I'd cared for it with every ounce of needing in my body. It had gone from stained and gutter-bound to inhabiting a place of pride tied around one of the bedposts in the house I shared with the love of my life. I'd explained the meaning and Bones understood. It didn't matter that I hadn't made the scarf, hadn't woven the fabric with my own fingers. Hadn't bought it new, taken a folded bundle of starch-stiff material from a shelf. "It's beautiful all the same." Maybe even more so to me.

Dogs are the same. My brain was trying to play catchup with my insides, following my heart down a path of what-ifs that was so wide with possibility it felt as if I'd never be lost again. There weren't any bad choices here, because everything was right. Sometimes the rehabbed dogs were the best ones. The ones who knew where they'd been, what they'd survived, and with hearts intact, they came out the other end with more love for people who cared. "I care. I could care a lot."

A child wasn't a dog, but I knew how twisted life could get for both. "They wouldn't have to be fresh and new." I could love them anyway. Would love them. *It. Him or her, whatever it was, there would be so much love.* I turned my head and looked through the house at the closed door, wanting to be as brave as Tiny was. This was big, and I wanted to tell Bones. Wanted him to know I'd come to here, now, today. And I was ready. "Doings. All the havings after. That's so big."

There was a cacophony in the house, the doorbell ringing startlement until I dropped my spoon. Bowl on the top of the table, me and the spoon underneath, I stared at the front door. Between the doorbell ringing loudly and Tiny barking hugely, boots scraping floors in a hurry, and even more motorcycles outside—I didn't want to move. When I glanced back at the window, the titmouse was gone. Unsurprised, I still hissed at his absence. "Traitor."

Then Shades was at the door, Bones' hand on Tiny's collar, holding him back, and Myron was striding in like he owned the world. Mindful of the playful hurt Bones had exposed the other night, I shot out from under the table and stopped by him first, tugging on his shirt until he bent sideways over the barking and lunging Tiny to kiss me. "Hush," I told Tiny, and he settled, leaning his big shoulder against Bones' leg.

I turned on my heel and ran towards Myron, seeing his face split in a big smile he only ever gave me. There he was, my Ronnie. He swung me in the air, and at the highest point, at the exact moment when my stomach rolled upwards to give me a weightless feeling, I saw Talya walking through the door, half hidden behind her father, Mouse. She was looking at me, then at Tiny, and then at Ronnie, not sure which of us to give her attention to.

My fists pounded on Ronnie's shoulders. "Put me down." I shot a quick look at Tiny, seeing in a moment how excited he was; muscles quivering, head down, tail up, he was ready for zoomies in a house that wasn't ready for that level of crazy. "Tiny," I barked at him in a voice he couldn't ignore. "Settle." Gunny had taught me that one. The word gave me just enough of a growl in my voice to make me unignorable, and Tiny's energy notched down by one. I considered him, then nodded, satisfied. Maybe two.

"Talya, this is Tiny." I reached out for her hand, seeing how Mouse's grip tightened for a moment, then relaxed. Simple trust in me given with love. *Oh, these men, they will be the death of my heart.* "I will never let anything hurt her." That was the most solemn promise I knew. "Ever." Mouse's eyes told me he believed me, but it might not be enough for true trust. "I would die first." Children were precious. He nodded, and I smiled, then knelt in front of Talya. "Tiny's big. You aren't. Until he knows you, I want you to stick tight to someone. It can be me, or your dad, or Myron." She nodded, then peered around me at the slobbering and panting beast still under Bones' hold. "Are you scared?" She nodded again. "Of what?"

"He could eat me."

"Negative. He likes dry dog food best." I laid her fear to rest as I shook my head. "What else?"

"He could bite me."

59

I made a clicking sound, considering. She was right and wrong in the same breath. "True, he's got teeth. But so do you. You could bite me. Why aren't you?" She tipped her head to the side. "Because you're a good girl." She nodded. "He's a good boy." I squeezed her hand. "What else?"

"He's so big and loud."

I cupped one hand around my ear and made a face I knew would make her laugh. It worked. He'd stopped barking immediately upon being told to and was waiting with huffed breaths to be allowed to meet the newest human in his pack. "He is? He's loud?"

"You know what I mean."

"He was loud when he didn't know who was behind the door. He can't help his bigness. That's just how his outsides are made. Like your outsides are still tiny. Tiny Talya, meet Big Tiny. His insides, though? He's not big at all." I stood and turned, then nodded at Bones. He relaxed his grip on Tiny's collar. "Tiny, come." Bones' hand opened, and head up, Tiny galloped towards me, ankles and elbows flying out to the side on the slick floors. "Tiny, sit." I'd gauged it right, because by the time he got his butt down and had stopped sliding, he was in a perfect sit directly in front of me, his laughing tongue exactly Talya tall. "Talya, this is Tiny." I introduced them again. "Tiny, this is Talya." He looked up at me, eyes wide and ears nearly brushing together over the top of his head as he listened. "She's important to me."

I touched her head, letting myself pet her hair. So soft and she smelled so good. My Ronnie was good to his girl, brushed the tangles out and got her girly shampoo. He'd told me once that she made his life more than he'd thought it could be. Caught midway between a little baby and a big girl, Talya was perfect for all the right reasons. I crooked an arm around her shoulders and gave her a sideways hug to thank her for making Ronnie happier than he expected to be.

"She's mine." Tiny's chin dropped at that and his eyebrows started their arguing dance. I shook my head and Talya giggled. "Yes, yes. If you're good, I promise I'll share her." He sighed, and his neck arched more, nose pointed at the ground. Tiny was pouting and I laughed. "He likes you." She giggled again as Tiny grumbled deep in his chest. Not a growl, not a bark, that was just him voicing his displeasure at being made to wait. "Stop complaining." Another grumble, and this one he chewed on, so the rolling sound came out chopped up as if he were saying "om, nom, nom," and Talya laughed, that sweet belling sound I'd loved so from the first time I'd heard it. Tiny seemed to feel the same way, because at her laughter he fell to his side, toppled by the force of her happiness. Feet flailing, he wormed his way along the floor until his head rested on her feet. "He likes you a lot."

"That's amazing." Mouse sounded confused and uncertain. "How did she do that?"

"It is my Ester's way. She charms children and dogs," Bones stepped towards me and bent his head to press a kiss against the side of my face. "And monsters."

***

Bones

With a tip of his head, Bones called the four men into the kitchen, leaving Ester to continue introducing Talya to the dog. He smiled as he gathered her dishes into the sink, because in his mind he could see exactly what she'd been doing. One of her favorite things, no matter the season, was to sit on the kitchen table and eat ice cream. He'd never gotten her to explain the why, and it didn't matter much. Whatever made Ester happy was permitted.

"Coffee?" He was already reaching for the canister as the men murmured behind him. "It is good you brought Talya, Myron. Thank you."

"Yeah, she'd be pissed at me if I didn't." Myron carried the milk from the refrigerator and set it on the counter next to the coffee machine. "She's so good with kids." He sighed heavily, and Mouse moved to stand beside him. "You'll let me know if there's anything I can do, right?"

Rage flowed through him for a moment, and before he could stop himself, Bones barked, "There will never be a day when I cannot care for Ester." He drew a breath and cut through the air with the edge of one hand. "My apologies, I know that was not what you meant to imply.

She is your sister, and what pains her also pains you. Of course, I will contact you if there is need." He turned and faced Myron. "It has only been a handful of months. She struggles with it, as you have seen. For me, she is enough. Always and until the end of my days, Ester will be all I need." He smiled, cocking his head down. "Needings."

"We've been brothers a while." Myron's tone was too casual, and Bones looked up to see the man was furious. As angry as Bones had been only moments ago. "But I tell you now, she's my sister, and I've just gotten her back. After years, it still feels like I've just gotten her back, and I won't let you put her mental health at risk because you were dealing with some kind of macho bullshit. She needs me, you pick up the goddamned phone." Feet spread wide, Myron shifted forwards an inch, chest stuck out, posturing in a way Bones didn't think he even knew he was doing. This was pure instinct, the drive of a man to protect those he loved, regardless the cost. "You got me?"

Bones stared at him for a moment, then nodded, their gazes still locked. "I understand you. Brother..." He pulled in a slow breath, feeling peace sweep through him at the acknowledgment of who they were to the other. "I got you. Your connection is not lost on me. And you know in your soul I would do anything for her. It is good she has men such as us at her back, yes?"

"Truth," Shades said, and Bones nodded, thankful for his interjection, because it would help relieve the still-tense situation. "That promised coffee ready yet, boss? Because I'd just like to point out how I'd been here nearly an hour before this pair showed, and you didn't offer me coffee. Not even a bottle of water. I don't rank as high as the brother-in-law. I see how you are."

Laughter around the room diffused the remaining tension, and Bones smiled as he nodded again. "That also is truth." He earned more laughter from them with his words, the sound echoing the bright laughter of Talya that trickled in from the other room. "What would your daughter like?" He gestured towards the refrigerator and watched as Mouse opened it and studied the contents. "There is some variety of juice drinks that Ester likes."

Mouse snorted. "My girl likes the same stuff. The sweeter the better." He raised his voice, calling out to the other room, "Hey, honey, you want cherry or grape juice?"

Bones laughed when two voices responded, both bright and cheerful, both laughing, and both exclaiming, "Purple, please."

"Tell me about the party." Myron lifted his mug to his lips, eyeing Bones over the rim. "What can I do?"

"You will be in Chicago that long?" The party was still two weeks away, so Myron's request was surprising.

"Maybe. We decided to hang out here for a bit. I haven't been around in too long, and Mouse and Talya have plenty of touristy stuff to do." Myron shrugged. "I thought I could spend some time with Ester." He took a drink, his face twisting as he fought some internal fight. "I gave you guys last year, but I wanted this Christmas to be...just, I wanted it to include me."

"I think you mean *we* gave you last year, allowing for the growth of your new relationship without intruding." Bones ignored Myron's smile, forging ahead and away from thoughts of family. "We have a number of children who will be at the party. If you stay, it would give Talya a chance to get to know her Chicago counterparts, too." Bones nodded. "What kind of help are you considering, Myron? We have a list, and there are ample things not yet crossed off."

"Whatever you need, brother." Myron made his way to the coffee machine again, refilling his mug. "Like I said, happy to help."

The doorbell rang. "I'll get it," Talya called. The floor thudded under Bones' feet, and he looked up in time to see Tiny trot into the kitchen, head high. He zeroed in on Bones and came to stand next to him, leaning heavily on the backs of his legs as the dog grumbled deep inside his chest. Tiny was pushing against him, shoving with a shoulder until Bones took a step sideways. "What, Tiny?" Somewhere over the past few days, he'd become a person who talked to dogs. Hand on the dog's head, he scratched roughly at the loose skin. "What is wrong?"

The doorbell rang again, but Tiny didn't charge or bark, just stayed next to Bones and pushed. That rough growl never ceased rolling up his throat, his body still shoving Bones sideways towards the front of the house.

Bones had a moment where things stopped in time, where he knew that whatever came next would be life-changing. He was in the last seconds of the before, and all that would exist from here out would be the after.

"Wait." The single word stuck in his throat, and he dropped his hand to Tiny's back. The dog's muscles were quivering. Then he heard a voice that surprised him. "Tater?" There was no danger his brother would bring to the household. Head cocked to the side, Bones listened to the sounds from the next room, hearing Tater and Talya holding a lively conversation, Ester's voice the most prominent absence. "Ester?" To Myron, he said, "Hold him," and led Tiny to him, putting the dog's collar in his hand.

"Ester?" He rounded the open archway and stepped into the living room that abutted the entryway. Ester was on her haunches, arms around Talya, who was looking up at Tater and Red curiously. "What is happening?"

"Bones," Tater said, and Red lifted his chin in greeting. "We've got a situation."

They stared at him, then looked at the office, and he understood what they wanted, but what he needed to know was what had happened to pull the blood from Ester's face. "Myron, Mouse, come here, please." Tiny didn't bark, but he did strip out of Myron's grip quickly, going to Ester and crowding in front of her and Talya, putting himself between them and the two men. For Tater and Red's benefit, he pointed towards the office with a nod. "Go. I will be with you momentarily."

Mouse stayed back, and Myron approached Ester as Bones did, slowly and quietly. Her head was tipped down now, face buried in Talya's neck so all he could see was the top of her head. "Talya," Myron called, holding out his hand, "come on, honey." She reached up and he gripped under her arms, lifting her from Ester's unresisting grip as she stayed on her knees. Tiny backed up and plunked his ass between Ester's legs, occupying the space where the little girl had been. He stared up at Bones, his ears and eyes conveying his worry.

"Ester, what has happened?" When she looked up at him, he froze in place, because the expression on her face was out of place for her reactions. It was filled with joy and happiness. "Ester?"

"I'll get it," she called, voice high and thready, exactly as Talya's had been. "Did you hear her? Bones, did you hear her?" He nodded and placed a hand on Ester's head, stroking her hair softly. "She's home, and you know what? We could have that. We could have a home like that. Where a tiny human wasn't afraid of answering the door, because it would never be the court lady coming to visit. Where a tiny human held music in her mouth, ready to give it to us whenever it made her happy. I was wrong, Bones." She stood and stepped around the dog to place her palms flat on his chest, face lifted to his, expression earnest. "I was wrong. It's in the doings. Not the things that come before. Sure, it matters, but does it matter more?" She shook her head, hair flying around, the brightness of her eyes still brightly visible. "No, it doesn't. That's what I realized outside, but then Red had to come visit for me to remember. It's in the doings we'd do together. I thought a pup would be good enough, and Tiny's good. But I wanna have a tiny human with you."

"Ester." He hated the pain in his voice, wished he could have hidden it more, but it was overwhelming him. His chest was tight with fear because she'd forgotten the raw truth and he would be the one to break her all over again. Telling her would break him, too. "Baby, please."

"No, not like that." She shook her head again, hair a wild cloud around her head. "I mean, how you said. The ways where not-me does the things that come before. Where the not-me has the swelled belly, and the sickness that comes and goes, and the blood and strain. But what *we* can do is all the doings after. You wanna do that with me?" Her voice dipped, became less confident and her eyes dimmed. "Bones, tell me. Did I miss it? Was it a one-and-done chance?"

He needed to be certain of what she meant, conscious of the uncomfortable audience they had—Red and Tater listening from the office doorway, Myron and Mouse only feet away. "Ester, my Ester. You and I cannot have a child of our own."

"False." Now she was pissed, and the glower she directed his way was scathing. "Am I yours?"

"Yes, of course you are."

"And are you mine?" He nodded, not sure where this was going now. "Why would a tiny human be different? You chose me, and I chose you, and if we choose a baby, a child, an infant, a tiny human—" She paused and took in a deep breath, her voice slow, testing each word as she spoke it when she finished. "—then why wouldn't that person be ours, just as we're each other's?"

Bones stared at her for a moment, seeing in her eyes the complex attention she'd given to thinking about the problem. Months, she must have been twisting it around in her head, trying to find a way through the snarled knot of pain and lost hopes. In the entirety of his life, he'd never wanted something as much as this, but he'd given up. Bones had thought she'd put it aside forever, but in true Ester fashion, she'd been thinking and considering, and waiting for the perfect time to tell him she was ready.

"You are right, my Ester. If we, if you and I, pick a child to be ours, then that is that. They will be ours."

"Forever." She waited, and he nodded. "No fear of being left behind. No fear of being alone. There'll be lots of days of 'I got it' for us." She sighed and leaned forwards, putting her forehead against his chest. "Thank you for being patient."

"For you, I find myself willing to do anything."

***

He settled a calm Ester with Talya and Mouse, then followed the other men into the office, smiling as Tiny forced his way in at the last moment. "Tell me," he said, turning from the door, "what is so urgent today." No smiles met his statement, which was surprising. The implication that the club always had business going on was not true, and normally Red would grin at the reminder of how things had slowed down. It was easier these days, and every man in the club breathed a little freer knowing it.

"We got a situation." Red held up his phone and passed it over. Myron stepped close to look over Bones' shoulder. "There's a video, then a couple of pics. Watch the vid first."

The still shot was a blurred shape in darkness, the triangle suspended over it, ready to be prompted to play. "What will I be looking at?" He didn't want to go into this without having at least an idea. "Give me something."

Tater spoke up, the expression on his face unreadable. "Bella's been trying to make friends. Your Ester, other old ladies like Red's." He swallowed. "The club whores, too. Not the party dolls, because I won't take her to those events. But residential gals, you know how it is. Old ladies can't help but know what they are when the gals are around the clubhouse all the time. So, Bella's made it a mission. That video is one Tawny sent her last night. Just watch it, brother. We need you to tell us what to do."

Bones nodded and a moment later, the sounds of a party filled the room. He studied the image on the phone, noting faces and location. "That is not our clubhouse." A statement, not a question, and he didn't look away from the screen to see their reaction. "These men, they are not Rebels. Where is this taken?" He sucked in a breath, because the video's perspective had floated high for a moment, looking down as if the person recording had their arms above their head, then had swooped down and came close to a woman's face. It took a moment, but the video finally focused in on her features. The sick feeling Bones had been fighting in the pit of his stomach grew stronger.

Unconscious, Tawny was laid out on what looked like a kitchen floor, arms and legs splayed. Based on the lack of tension in her limbs, he assumed she was not restrained. There were only a few more seconds, and on the video nothing untoward was happening, but he could see her clothing had been wrenched awry, seams popped along her shoulder. Her face was bruise-free, and blissed out, which meant "She is high."

"Yeah." Red met Bones' gaze. "I'd noticed she was wearin' sleeves lately, but didn't think anything of it; it's winter. But then I saw that vid. Watch it again, and look closely at her arms, Bones. I think she's usin'."

"Where was this taken?" He rewound the video to the best angle on her arms, then shook his head. "It is not clear. I will not accuse someone based on an anonymous video. What did she say when you questioned her?" He held the phone out to Red, but Myron intercepted the handoff, taking the phone over by the desk. Bones ignored what he was doing, knowing Myron would have a better version of the video before this conversation was over. "She is ours, but she knows she cannot live in the clubhouse if she is using." He didn't have to say it, because every man in the room knew, but the club would send her to a clinic if needed. They'd done it before with mixed results. For Tawny, who had lived at the clubhouse for more than fifteen years, it would not even be a question. "We detox her and rehab."

"Can't find her." Tater shook his head. "Bella tried all the other gals, and no one's seen her."

"Or they are not talking," Bones interjected, but Tater shook his head. "You think Bella has earned their trust that well?"

"I do. She's had girl dates with them. They like her, but more, they trust her. She told them there'd be no blowback for telling on Tawny, but they don't know anything. She told me they were worried, too." He shrugged. "As to where that footage was taken, I don't have the faintest clue. It could be anywhere, Bones."

"She has a room at the clubhouse." Not a question, but Red still nodded. "Search it. Turn it upside down. Look everywhere we know are hiding places. Look where *we* would hide something like that. Toss it and tell me what is found."

Myron looked up. "Mouse and me are headed to the clubhouse in a few. We were going to take Talya. Want to come along with Ester?"

Bones considered for a moment, then nodded. "Two birds, one stone. If we find anything, I will call Mason from there. And" —he smiled at the men— "I can ask Ester to check on the party plans. See if she will engage. It would be good."

An hour later, he rolled his eyes as he parked their car next to the clubhouse building. Hot, heavy breathing echoed in his ear, and if he moved his head too far to the side, he knew he risked a tongue lashing. Again.

"Tell me why Tiny needed to come?" Ester giggled, and he smiled. He would do much for that sound. "Never mind, it does not matter. We are here now. Do you want me to take his leash?"

"No, I've got it. Him. I'm good." She blew out a huff of air, stirring the bangs that dropped back over her eyes. "I know people here."

"You do." He reassured her, sitting still behind the wheel until she gave him the signal to get out. If she was unsettled, he would wait with her. "Myron and Mouse, Talya, Red, Tater and Bella, Shades." He glanced around the lot. "Plowboy and Road Runner."

She nodded jerkily. "I'm good. I know all of *them*." When one hand lifted to scratch absently along Tiny's jaw, she muttered, "Tiny's here, too. And you are. My Bones." She cut her gaze towards him, then back towards her knees. "You're here. That's the most important parts of the whole dealiebob. You being here. With me. You wanting me here with you. My Bones. I can do anything with you."

"You can do anything, period." She shivered, and he placed his palm on her thigh, stroking reassuringly. Tiny whined and pressed hard against her hand. "You have always been amazing to me."

"Okay." She sat still for a moment longer, then gripped the door handle tightly. "Tiny, wait." The dog grumbled, chewing at the sounds until they were nearly words, and Bones laughed at the idea of him talking. Ester frowned, then giggled. "Hush, both of you."

He met her at the door leading inside and halted her with a hand at her waist. He angled his head down, knuckle under her chin to lift her mouth, and kissed her. Deep, long strokes of his tongue against hers, teeth nipping at her lips, he kissed her until her breath came fast. "Do you know how much I love you?" Without opening her eyes, she smiled and nodded, looking drunk on the kiss. "Double that. My love has grown."

Slow blinks parted her lids, and her eyes sparkled as she looked up at him. "That's a lot." He nodded, slipping that knuckle along the edge of her jaw in a slow caress. "Backatcha, mister."

Inside, Ester stuck by his side only a moment before Talya and Bella peeled her away, Tiny going along with her. The backwards glance she gave him made his heart skip, but the tender way she cuddled the little girl into her side started an ache in his belly he couldn't wait to explore. With everything that had happened after the men had gotten to his house, Bones hadn't nearly enough time to digest the change in direction Ester was dictating. Her reasoning was spot-on, and he understood how she'd gotten there, but after not believing it was in the cards for them, Bones was off balance in all the right ways to have it dangled in front of him suddenly.

Bones made his way to the bar, standing near the end beside the door to the office. He saw Myron inside, working on a computer. "You are still digging into the video?" Myron nodded and lifted a bottle without looking up, taking a deep pull of beer. "Let me know when you have something." Myron nodded again, and

Bones turned to accept a bottle from the prospect manning the bar. With Myron, it would be when, not if, and Bones knew whatever was found would be more than expected when Myron did hand it over. "Red," he called and jerked his head. The minute the paramedic was close enough, he asked, "Her room?"

"Tater's headed up in a minute. He decided to do it and not assign it out. That way if nothing's found, it's not a black mark against Tawny."

Bones lifted his beer and took a drink, then said, "He will come get us if he needs to."

"Yeah. He's as anti-hard stuff as any of us are. I think he's feeling guilty because with Tawny spending time with Bella, he thinks he should have seen it sooner." Red shrugged. "If it's true, then there's no blame for any one man. We'd all shoulder it. Addicts, though." He sighed. "They're damn good at hiding shit."

"Boss." Bones jerked his gaze up the stairs to see Tater already gesturing him up.

"Fuck," he muttered and set the bottle on the bar, swept the area to verify Ester's safety and well-being, then took the steps two at a time. "What?"

"She's…" Tater rubbed a rough hand over his head, fingers tangling in his hair. "It's bad, Bones."

Striding down the hallway to where the few residential apartments were, he stopped in front of the only one with a closed door. Arching an eyebrow in a silent question, he got a nod from Tater. Hand to the knob, he turned it and pushed, keeping his feet outside the room until he could get a look at what had Tater so spooked. It wasn't hard to see, because Tawny lay on the floor next to the bed. Even without the fresh track marks trailing up her arm, the visibly gray tint to her skin told the gruesome tale. The rancid stench of vomit tainted the air, and Bones looked around to see her kit on the floor next to the dresser. There was a box half pushed underneath, and he suspected when examined, they would find whatever stash she had left tucked inside.

"Fuck." Bones stared at her, remembering all the times he'd seen her around the clubhouse. Years of her life spent here, surrounded by men who liked her, but didn't love her. She'd looked for it, too. But she'd also looked for friends. He remembered Gypsy's story about her using him as a haven, and that wasn't the only member who had protected her in that way, giving her a safe place to lay her head until Bones had ordered a dedicated room be made available to her. A space in their house that was solely hers. *She's earned it*—that's what he'd told Red at the time, and the man knew Bones wasn't talking about working on her back. She'd earned it through her loyalty and support of the club.

He swallowed hard. "Did she have family?"

Myron's voice sounded from a distance up the hallway. "Ester, hold on. No, honey." Bones felt the rapid tattoo of Tiny's stride through the soles of his boots, and knew his woman would be chasing his dog.

He wasn't quick enough to derail Tiny's fast entrance into the room; the dog ducked his hand and skidded past, slippery as an eel. Ester was right behind the dog, and Bones stopped her with an arm around her shoulders. "No, baby. This is not for you." Tiny barked loudly, the sound echoing out of the room. Bones turned his head, expecting to see the dog barking at Tawny, but he was angled towards the closet instead, gaze focused on the closed door. "Myron, please." Ester's hands fell away from his waist where she'd been gripping his belt, and he turned, striding into the room.

He studied the dog for a moment, then pulled his gun from the hidden holster at his back. He glanced back to see Red and Tater crowding the door, but Ester was in front of them. She was staring at Tiny, not seeming to notice the body on the floor. "Get her out, please." He turned back to the closet and jerked the door open, then froze in place.

Tiny didn't suffer the same impediment, bounding forwards with high-pitched whines. Chest to the floor, his ass was lifted high, tail whipping back and forth. He had his nose running along a small pair of arms holding skinny knees against a slender chest. Head bowed, face buried, the only thing visible from the top was a mass of red-gold hair, curling into an untidy mess. Tiny poked again, his entire head disappearing under the wave of hair, and then Bones heard the giggle. Soft and quiet, but somehow so bright it lit up the entire room.

"Oh." Ester pushed past him, carelessly shoving his weapon to the side as she fell to her knees. "Tiny, what did you find me today?"

Bones stared at her for a moment, then tucked the unneeded gun back into its holster. The child, because surely it was one, had hair the exact shade as the dead woman. *Fuck*.

Ester cooed, "Tiny, you're such a good finder." More giggles, then the head covered in tawny hair lifted, and he saw the most beautiful pair of blue-gray eyes he'd ever seen staring up at him. They held his gaze for a moment, then turned their attention to Ester sitting on the floor with her legs crisscrossed. "There you are." A yip from Tiny, who was now lying on his side across the little girl's feet. "That's Tiny. He's a doof today. I'm Ester." A pause, then Ester asked, "Do you have a name?" The child shook her head, gaze darting back and forth from Ester to Tiny. "That's okay. Some names take longer to find. Those are the big ones."

The big dog rolled to his back, wrestling with what might have been a white cotton ball, if Bones hadn't seen the button black eyes and nose, lip lifted to show tiny white teeth, nipping at Tiny's nose again.

"What the fuck just happened?"

Chapter Four

Bones

"She had no family? There is no one?" Dismissive shakes from around the table made Bones lower his head to his closed fist again. They were in the clubhouse meeting room, the connecting door to the larger main area closed. Ester and the little girl were out there with a dozen trusted people, and Bones was in here, trying to make sense of everything that had happened. Eyes closed, he rubbed his thumb across his forehead. "Did any member know of the girl?"

At the continued silence he lifted his head, pinning each man in turn with a glare. "No one?"

"Not so far," Red said with a shrug. "About four years ago, she came to me for a morning-after pill. I got what she needed, and she didn't say anything else. I assumed what anyone would, Bones."

"Someone had to have seen, or noticed when she was carrying the child." He shook his head, angry at the idea that Tawny had been so invisible to all of them. Much as homeless people were in the city, commuters striding past on their way to the next moment of their orderly lives. *Much as Ester had been*, he thought. *But I saw her*. No one, it seemed, had *seen* Tawny. "A child and a dog, and an addict."

Myron rested his hand on the table, palm flattened. "People get caught up in their own lives, brother. It's not a failing; it's just a fact. If she'd wanted to be caught, she would have been. Clearly she wanted to keep secrets." Inside the closet, they'd found a tiny pallet of blankets for the child. A small shelf had been stocked with easy-open toddler food, something the girl should have outgrown by now, but it was tasty and relatively cheap. Dog food was in an airtight container, and as growly and fierce as the puppy had seemed, he hadn't barked yet. Not even when prompted to by Tiny, who had latched onto the tiny fluffball much as Ester had the child.

"We callin' a bus?" Red's question was quiet but held a lot of pain. Bones studied him a moment. "Just seems wrong, leavin' her lyin' on the floor."

"We call an ambulance, we might as well swing the doors open for LEO." Bones shook his head. "We need to find an alternate location to arrange for her discovery. I will not risk the club. If she were yet alive and fighting, yes, brother, we would have made that call before anything else. But she overdosed in our clubhouse, and the first thing LEO will assume is the drugs were a result

80

of her residence here. I know different, and so do you, but we are not fools, you and I. We have been through similar processes before, and know the authorities are quick to dig in, but slow to retract their claws."

"I know, Bones. It just ain't right." Red gritted his teeth as he snarled silently. "It's gonna eat at me, so let's make some decisions here."

"We are agreed on most, and I will handle the details on Tawny." Bones skimmed the top of the table with his hand, back and forth, as if sweeping crumbs together. "We know there was no wrongdoing, and we'll ensure she's found quickly. But what of the girl?" Silence and head shaking from around the table. "Tawny was RWMC. She belonged to us." More silence. "Is that not true?"

"No. I mean, yeah, you've got the right of it, Prez." Tater pressed his lips together tightly. "Just, what are we gonna do with a little girl? We don't know if she's got family or anything." Even before he said the next words, Bones read what would be suggested, and in his gut, he knew he wouldn't allow it. Couldn't. Not knowing what Ester had gone through. "CPS would be the best place to start."

He stared at Tater, then looked at Shades and Myron, both of whom had experiences with the system. Myron from the inside, much as Ester had, and Shades when he rescued his brother's orphaned children from an abusive foster home. "Child Protective Services is understaffed." He took a breath. "There are well-meaning people within their ranks, but we are not guaranteed this child would be assigned to such." He shook his head. "We have the benefit of our expert and resident geek. Why should we not try to surface such relatives as this little girl might have ourselves?"

Myron's head jerked up, and he nodded quickly, eyes going round. "I don't need much, brother. I can get a start with Tawny's info."

"Make it so." Bones lifted the gavel and brought it down once. "I will pay respect to Tawny in the only way left to me."

Chairs scuffed across the wooden floor as the men pushed back from the table one by one. Bones stayed seated, chin propped on his clasped fingers, elbows to the surface. He stared absently, eyes not focused on the scarred table. Instead, his mind alternated between two things. His thoughts bounced back and forth from the memory of seeing Tawny on the floor, dead, in *his* house, under *his* care, on *his* watch...and how Ester had looked as she sat in front of the little girl, eyes bright, shielding the child from seeing her mother by deftly boxing her in with her body, the enormous Dane and miniscule puppy wrestling between them.

It didn't matter to Ester who the girl was, who she belonged to, or why she was there. All she knew was the potential disaster, and she'd moved to derail it, protecting the girl. The same thing she'd done with every child he'd ever seen in her presence, how she was with the dogs at the rescue, and more especially with Tiny. Myron hadn't skimped on his story of how she'd reamed the man who'd called, and from how she'd acted on the phone, speaking confidently into the device for the first time he could ever remember, Bones believed every word.

She's strongest when she has something to protect. He swallowed hard. "Ester has good instincts."

Myron cleared his throat. "Yeah, she does."

"That child cannot go into the system. That is one of Ester's worst fears." He didn't shift, didn't change position, muscles vibrating with the need to hurt someone because of the things Ester had survived. In the past, but present in the way she still ached over the betrayals. "She still dreams of it, you know? The things that went on behind her foster family's door." His hands gave a twinge of pain, and he realized he'd been tightening his fingers, over and over, clenching down. "They are not good dreams, Myron. I cannot—" His voice broke and he stopped, struggling for a moment to regain control. "CPS cannot have her."

"What are you gonna do?" Red asked from the doorway, hovering, probably waiting to assist with the removal of Tawny's body.

Bones looked up finally, locking eyes with Myron as he answered his long-time friend, his brother, one of a handful of men he trusted with his life. "Ester needs a child to be whole. If you do not find a loving father waiting in the wings…if you do not find a family that deserves her, then that child will be ours." Myron shook his head and Bones shoved the chair back, fists propped on the table as he leaned across, jutting his chin out aggressively. "Do not naysay me on this, brother. You find a worthy family, then I will say and do no more. But if that child needs us, we will not turn her away. And I will lean on whomever I must to make it happen."

"Brother." Red's voice held caution, and Bones swung to face him. "You can't promise something like this to Ester, not if there's a chance of taking it back. You can't do that to her, man."

"You think I do not know my own woman?" Drawing himself up to his full height, he stared at the man. "I would sooner cut my own tongue out than make promises to her such as that. Do not count me as a fool, Red."

"No fool, but you want something bad enough, it's easy to get ahead of the process." Red shook his head. "Just…come see this, brother." He waved towards the open doorway beside which he stood, gesturing out into the main clubhouse room. "Come see."

Bones made his way around the table, stepped up beside Red, and locked in place. The meeting had been longer than expected, and what greeted him was a vision he'd never once allowed himself to imagine.

Ester lay lengthwise on a couch, a blanket thrown over her legs, head on a pillow someone had brought from upstairs. Between her and the back cushions was the child, her head nestled on Ester's shoulder, their hair spreading together into an unruly heap. Tiny had made himself small enough that he could rest on the other end of the couch, while the white puppy curled up on top of his feet. The Great Dane's head was laid on top of Ester's leg, and Ester's arm thrown over the child, so they were all connected.

His heart stuttering in his chest and throat tight, he told Red, "I see. Oh, brother, I see."

***

Ester

I woke with a creaky neck and Bones' lips on mine, so I counted it good. "My Ester," he said to me, and I wasn't done tasting him yet, so I stretched upwards until he kissed me again, chuckling against my mouth. That counted as better.

"Hey." My response wasn't pithy, or smart, but he smiled at me and that spot just in the center of my everything warmed.

"You have a friend." He tipped the top of his head to the back of the couch, and I angled my head to see her. Still sleeping, which was good. She'd been scented by exhaustion when I'd picked her up from the floor of the closet earlier. I'd fed her, and helped wash her hands and face, but the smell of soured sweat and hunger still clung to her skin. "Do you know her name?"

Eyes still on the small girl, I shook my head. She'd been quiet, too quiet, a silence I knew too well weighing on her tongue to keep it from moving. Her not telling wasn't a malicious thing, and I wanted Bones to know so he kept looking at her with those warm eyes. "She didn't lie. She just didn't speak."

"Most likely she has been through a lot." I tipped my head back to look at him. His mouth twitched, but not in a smile, which meant he was measuring his words for the right fit. "Do you think she had been here for long, Ester?"

"I don't know. Why don't you ask me what you want to ask? Stop waiting. Just ask. I won't break, Bones." His caution made me angry as it hadn't done before. "Give it to me. Come on."

"Ester." He shook his head slowly. "You saw her mother."

The memory hit me then, the reason I'd run to the tiny human. I'd smelled the death in the room, smelled it and chased Tiny, thinking that was what he wanted to protect. A dead woman who didn't need anyone's protection anymore. Then I'd heard the sound. Heard her. Lilting on the air like birdsong, and I'd had to see. Had to see and keep safe, because as brilliantly sweet and innocent as the giggle had been, I knew the person who produced it was the same.

"I wanted to keep her from changing." I'd seen dead people before, lots of times. It was a rite of passage for street people, ever-worsening tales told over trash can fires deep in the bitterest winters. "I didn't want her to carry that with her forever."

"But you understand, yes?" His hand coasted across my cheek, fingers pushing into my hair to cradle the back of my skull. "If her mother was all she had, then things are…" He measured his words again, lips moving sideways twice before he found the right one. "Precarious."

"I know you." He blinked. "I trust you." *With my life*, I told him with my eyes. "You've never failed me." I rolled my head to look at the girl, and found her blinking sleepily at me. "You won't fail now."

***

We sat on the floor of Bones' study, she and I. We and the pups, and Bones behind the desk. He worked at the computer and was wordless. The only sounds in the room were the gigantic breaths Tiny kept huffing at the furiously growling puppy, and that quiet, rhythmic tapping of the keyboard.

She handed me the sock toy back, and I watched the puppy's eyes track it from her hands to mine. Dangling one end in front of his nose, it wasn't but a moment when he took the bait and lunged upwards with a fierce grrr, teeth latched into the stretchy fabric. On his feet, spine bowed, he jerked backwards with a series of grunted growls, each breathier than the next.

"Oh, he's a fierce one." The little girl nodded, her eyes on Tiny. I glanced his way to see a version of his happiest face, doggy grin wide with his broad tongue lolling over his teeth. "That's Tiny," I reminded her, and she nodded. "What's the pup's name?" She ducked her chin to her chest, hair falling over her face. Instead of trying to pry it out of her, which would surely be impossible if she were as stubborn as I was at that age, I decided to run a different route.

"Buttons." Head tilted to the side, I grinned at the pup who hadn't ceased in his efforts to dislodge my hold on the sock toy. *He's as stubborn as she is.* "His nose is black, and his eyes are dark. They look like buttons." From the corner of my eye, I saw the head shake, vehement in her refusal of that name for her pup. "Okay, not Buttons. It can be hard sometimes to find a heart-name for someone."

"Heart-name?"

I heard Bones' indrawn breath, but I didn't respond to him. She'd asked her question, and I'd give it the right weight of consideration. "Yeah, the name inside that's the truest of things for them. People have them; dogs have them." I flicked a finger behind me towards Bones. "That man? His heart-name is Bones. His friends think it came from a silly game. A saying uttered once and forgotten by most. But the truth, his heart-truth? Bones is Bones because he is the solid framework of everything needed, slowly built up layer by layer. A framework he put in place to protect people he loves." I tugged at the sock toy, dragging the puppy back towards me by a couple of feet, grinning when he growled louder at the loss of progress. "He loves me. I'm his Ester."

There was silence in the room from all the humans for a minute, and Bones started tappity tapping on the keys again. "Puffball." I snaked the sock toy back and forth, playing whip with the puppy as a movable anchor. Tiny thudded a foot on either side of the small dog, helping him not slide so far. "Cheater," I complained to him, and he panted dog breath in my face. "Ox. He's stubborn as one. Does that fit him?"

I rocked backwards as the puppy let go suddenly, the volume of his growling growing. He was tucked under Tiny's chin, peering at me from that dubious safety. "Okay, not Ox. Jeez." I passed the sock toy back to the little girl and bent my legs double, tight to my chest, chin on my knees. "So far we've a lot of nots." She giggled and held up the sock toy, composed entirely of knotted single socks, mismatched in such a way that they matched perfectly. "A lot of knots." I laughed. "Touché, which does not mean to touch." She dangled the toy in front of Tiny, who took the tip of the fabric between his front teeth, tossing his head carefully to pull just enough. She nearly toppled over and he dropped it, his eyebrows getting lost in the shadows of his ears, drawn up on top of his head in concern. Laughing, she whipped the sock away and gave it to the puppy, who settled between Tiny's legs. One of the pup's white feet rested on top of Tiny's, and I laughed at the difference. "He's so small. Small, but fierce." She nodded and lay down, her head on Tiny's flank. He stared at me. "I know," I told him. "I like them, too." He and I sighed in sync, and I laughed. The pup's eyes were active as he chewed on the socks, darting from dog to person to dog to thing to dog. "You're going to see everything eventually. There's no rush. You're here with us now."

"Tiger." She popped her thumb out of her mouth to give me his name, and I took that with careful attention, knowing what it meant that she'd gifted us so.

"Tiger." I breathed the name out and felt how right it was. He might be small, might be not even half grown, but his heart was big. He'd tried to keep Tiny away from the girl until he got to know the Dane's heart. Just like Tiny was big outside, but his inside was wary and submissive. "Oh yeah. I see it. Tiger is perfect. You already knew his heart-name. He's so big inside; it doesn't matter what his outsides are." I petted her hair, angling around to lean against Bones' desk with my back. Tiny stretched out a foot and put it on my leg. The only thing missing was...I reached high, waving my hand over my head, and a moment later, strong fingers folded around mine. "We're all perfect just how we are."

***

Bones

The chill woke him, and Bones opened his eyes, reaching to the side to find Ester gone. He listened closely and could hear sleeping breaths from Tiny, wedged against the door as the dog did every night. An early warning system he hadn't expected. Ester's breathing was in the room, too, but not sleeping. Quick and light, each respiration told him she was awake and aware, but closer to the floor than the mattress. He rolled to the edge and looked down.

One of the heavy blankets from their bed had been spread across the floor, and Ester lay on it, one edge of the cover curled up over her hip and across the girl sleeping in front of her. He saw the glinting dark eyes of the puppy, Tiger. Then the animal laid its head back down, having deemed him no threat.

Ester's hand moved slowly, rhythmically, fingers working through the little girl's hair. He wasn't surprised to see them, not really. The child had gone to sleep in the spare bedroom just up the hall, but had looked lost on the wide mattress. The bed too high for her pup to jump up, Bones had lifted him to her, earning a nip on the finger for his efforts. Ester had planted herself inside the room until she'd nearly been sleeping standing up and he'd forced her to their bed.

They still had no name for the child.

Myron had uncovered exactly no birth records, which was surprising.

Tawny's body had been recovered by the authorities, and she was in the morgue now, cared for as best as she could be given the situation. If no autopsy was ordered, the club would pay to have her cremated, and Bones would pick up the box of ashes in a week or so. He'd already decided to store it until the girl was old enough to decide what to do with her mother's remains.

Ester had discovered the girl's favorite foods, and he'd ordered a mass delivery of oriental dishes like she'd described. Then the girl had surprised again, because even as hungry as she looked, cheeks gaunter than he wanted to see, limbs thin, she'd shown restraint in her selection of foods and portions. That likely had more to do with discipline than with manners, because when Ester had noted what the girl favored from the assortment, she'd piled more on the child's plate. He'd laughed when her little eyes grew round, mouth opening slightly in shock, and then she'd flashed a smile at Ester before digging in.

Each thing the little girl did hooked deeper into his heart. Too trusting, but she was a child after all. It tore at his mind to think of her in another's hands. She'd come with them without question, not once asking after her mother, only ensuring they'd brought her dog's things along. On the short ride from the clubhouse to their home, he'd watched in the mirror as the girl turned to check on her puppy's toys and dishes a dozen times, ignoring the bag that held her few possessions.

Red had come by during dinner, carrying a duffle stuffed to bursting with clothing to fit, winnowed from a stash his old lady had in the attic. Ester had wrinkled her nose and dumped it all in the washer, shaking copious amounts of detergent in on top. Once they were out of the dryer and she'd been satisfied, Ester had sat and clapped with each wardrobe change, the little girl darting in and out of the hallway bathroom, clothes clutched in her hands.

It has only been hours, he reminded himself. Myron still had a chance of locating someone who had a stake in the girl. If they were good people, she'd do best with family. Blood. His heart whispered, *She'll do well here.*

Without lifting her head, Ester whispered, "I don't want it back."

"What, my love? What do you not want back?" He reached down and stroked her hair, matching her movements with the child.

"My heart. She took it clean out of my chest, Bonesy. Easiest thing in the world." She sniffed quietly, but he heard the thick in her throat when she said, "She's the most perfect of anything. It was scary for her here, but she came to me when it drove her out of bed. Floors are comfortable when that's what you're used to, so I left you there." Another sniff. "I'm sorry."

"Shhhh. You did exactly right, my Ester. In my eyes you are the most perfect of anything, and that is what you have given her." He shook his head. "I did not think how the bed might seem. So big and tall, and she is so small."

"She's big on the inside. She and Tiger, they're a match." She pulled in a deep breath, shoulders hitching twice as she settled closer to the child. "She's a match."

Red's words came back to him, and he tried to hold tight to caution. Still, Ester deserved to know he understood, and was of the same mind. "I cannot guarantee you anything, Ester. There are too many unknowns at this point. But if I can, I will. I promise you that. If I can, I will, because she fits."

"She does." Ester rolled her head and looked up at him from her position on the floor. She hesitated a moment, then told him, "I love you the same. Every day is Bonesday in my heart."

"Things like this do not divide love. They multiply it." He slipped half off the bed, bracing himself with an arm beside her head as he dipped low to touch his mouth to hers. "I love you more."

Ester sighed against his lips; then he felt them move under his kiss and knew she was smiling. "Bring another blanket when you come."

Without hesitating, he reached behind him and gripped the comforter, dragging it to cover the three of them as they lay in the nest Ester had created on the floor. He tucked his arm around Ester's belly, felt the heat of the child's back against his arm and shifted his hold to include her, too. Something moved under the blankets and he froze, then felt the sting of tiny teeth on his toe dig deep before releasing, the furry ball of heat curling around his feet. It seemed Tiger had found his sleeping place for the night.

"Good night, Bonesy."

Ester stiffened against him and he smiled.

That hadn't been her voice, pitched quiet and high. That graceful lilt that had filled the air and made him lighter just by hearing it…belonged to the little girl.

Chapter Five

Bones

"No, there has been no word on our side." It had been three days since Tawny's child had been discovered living in a closet in the clubhouse, and they were no closer to knowing anything about her. "You have exhausted options with her family, then?"

Myron was on video today, having decided to take his family back to Fort Wayne for the holidays. There was too much going on here to have the kind of visit he had wanted. But Bones knew Myron hadn't stopped searching. The list of dead ends he'd already recited testified to that. He shook his head. "No, I found a sister, but she's dead. Parents are both dead. There's literally no one else who could have a claim on that little girl. With no birth record, and nothing even in the private midwives' database fitting the timeframe I've isolated, it's like the child just materialized out of thin air."

"You are frustrated." Myron tipped his head back at Bones' words. "It is not a bad thing, Myron. That just says you care. Maybe too much." He winced at the death glare received through the camera. "Have you given thought to her using an alias? Tawny's government name was memorable enough; perhaps she chose something else to hide behind?"

"Carson DeLauro. I'd say that's unique." Myron studied a paper in his hand. "Sister's name was Carlton."

"When did the parents pass?" Bones wasn't focusing in on anything, but from years of working with him, he knew how Myron's brain was wired. If he could maneuver him into looking at random things associated with what he needed to solve, it kept his active mind busy, while his subconscious kept picking at the puzzle.

"Eight years ago. It was sudden. The club helped with expenses."

Bones vaguely remembered something about it. "It was a car crash, yes?"

Myron nodded. "On the Dan Ryan. Wintertime. Slippery as snot, and cars didn't have any business on the roads. They slid into the back of another vehicle already crashed."

"No grandparents, aunts, or uncles?" Myron shook his head. "The sister, Carlton. When did she die?"

Myron consulted another paper, then brought his computer in front of him to type something on the screen. Bones waited. "Four months ago." There was a tone in his voice Bones knew well. A vibration that said Myron had caught wind of something that mattered. More rapid typing, and then an inrush of breath. "Jesus. And not quite five years ago, she gave birth to a little girl, father unknown."

"Is there a paper trail from the sister to Tawny for the girl?" He didn't doubt for a moment that she was Tawny's niece, not daughter. It matched the known details too well, much better than Tawny having a child of her own. "Were the courts involved?" Tawny had a will that said everything she had went back to the club. Red had found it when cleaning her things out of the bedroom. A club attorney had drawn it up, and when they checked with him, found it was still in effect. "I know a little girl is not a thing, not a possession, but if there is documentation, it would be good to know now." Something hit him, and he ground his teeth, holding his silence for a moment. He could know. Only moments from now, he could know and then take it to Ester. "Myron, show me the birth certificate. Please."

In response, Myron tapped something and the view changed, showing the computer screen. There were dozens of windows, websites, and folders Myron had open, but the mouse clicked one of them, and then it grew to take over the entire width. It moved up, then down, and then stopped. His disembodied voice asked, "There, that's what you wanted, right?"

Bones didn't voice a response, just nodded. On the screen was a copy of a document. Stamped with the seal from the Illinois Department of Vital Records, it had several lines of information.

Infant girl born to Carlton DeLauro on January 16, at 3:32 a.m. Weighing 6 pounds 12 ounces, she had measured an even 21 inches.

Essence Rena DeLauro.

My little girl is nameless no more. Bones didn't even flinch at the possessive thoughts. He just stared at the name, etching it onto his memories. "Essence." He closed his eyes and blew out a quick breath. "Brother." When he looked back at the screen, the document was gone, and Myron's attention was on him. "Find what you can. This, though, this is not bad news."

Without shutting down the computer, he turned towards the door, shouting, "Ester. Where are you?"

Without even a second thought, he closed the study door on the sound of Myron's laughter.

***

Ester

Essence and I sat on the edge of the kitchen table, bowls in hand, eyes fixed on the birds outside.

"Tomorrow's Christmas." I sighed. Her feet kicked back and forth, covered by the smallest pair of my socks. Now hers. "You can keep those." I pointed my spoon toward her feet. She looked at me with a tiny smile and nodded shyly before shoving another spoonful of ice cream into her mouth.

She was still quiet, and I tried to explain to Bones the why of it all. So much had happened to her in such a short time, it would have seemed everything was out of her control, so she took hold of what she could, spending her words carefully. We knew from headshakes and nods, from smiles and frowns, that she hadn't known her aunt before Tawny showed at the hospital to take her home. Too young to understand death, she'd looked for her mother everywhere they went, and still looked in the oddest of places, just for reassurance that she hadn't missed seeing her mom under the couch, in the cabinets, or in the laundry hamper.

Her mother had been murdered, so my Ronnie was looking into things. He and Bones had been careful with the details around me, not understanding that I didn't care. I did not care what had happened in the past, except where it could stop things from happening today. I realized a long time ago that the only thing I knew was I loved Bones, and Bones loved me.

And now I could add the realness of love for Essence. Even her name was perfect, because she was the heart of rightness in this house. *Our house*. Since she'd come home with us, the place had seemed more real than before, more his and mine and hers and ours, and I was home. I was home, and so was she.

"You're staying here."

She nodded, the metal edge of her spoon scraping along the bottom of the bowl, gathering up the final smears of sweet, creamy goodness.

"We're home." I held out my hand for her empty bowl, taking it and placing it on the table behind us. Her legs swung, back and forth, and back, left leg getting out of sync with the right for a swing or four, then easing into rhythm again. She leaned against me, and I rested my elbow on her head, dishing up the last bite.

"You want this?" I brought the spoon down in front of us, and in the reflection, I saw her little mouth open like a baby bird, trusting me to provide for her. Lips closed around the spoon, she pretended to growl like Tiger, clamping her teeth to pull it from my fingers. My laughter brought Tiny and Tiger running, the white puffball winding through the rangy limbs of the Great Dane, both managing to make their way to us without painful incident.

Essence grinned up at me, lips parting around the stem of the spoon still in her mouth. "Watch this," I told her and grabbed the spoon from her bowl. I licked the inside and stuck it to the end of my nose, then held my hands out to the side like a magician doing a big reveal. Her eyes went round and she tried to emulate me, giggling when her spoon fell off time and again. "Want to know the secret?" She nodded. "Lick it." I showed her again, and then we were sitting on the kitchen table staring out at the backyard, reflection in the windows catching the glint of the suspended spoons.

"What are my girls doing?" Bones' voice came from behind us, but neither Essence nor I jumped. It was our home, after all. Plus, I'd seen him in the reflection. I'd watched as he paused for a long moment in the doorway, the fractured expression on his face readily readable to me. *Love.*

"Watching." Essence's head bobbed, hair brushing against my arm. I'd braided it for her last night before bed, and she'd been amazed at the tangle-free condition this morning. Now it was wild again, puffing up and out after a long day of freedom. "Tiny's birds. I feeded them."

"And then you ate ice cream." I loved that there was no judgment in his voice, no anger at spoiling her supper. Even without knowing how hard she'd run and played in the backyard, which would mean her appetite could stand a tiny treat, he didn't aim any barbs of disapproval towards me. "I am chef tonight." He leaned against my back, one arm beside me, one beside Essence. He kept his attention on her while he placed soft kisses up my neck. "I shall make lasagna." Another kiss, followed by a nudge of his nose to turn my head. I surrendered to him, placing my lips against his for a sweet, short but deep kiss that would have made my legs weak if I weren't already sitting. "My girls can keep watching."

I saw her reflection move, chin lifting in a clear demand he didn't ignore. Bones placed a sweet, short and loud kiss on her forehead. Essence and I laughed at the smack, and Tiny whined piteously, the sound trailing on and on.

"No, Tiny. I did not forget you." Bones went to the cabinet where we kept the treats, taking out a handful. Then he was cursing and moving back, the room filled with vicious-sounding growls. "Dammit, Tiger." I turned to watch as the tiny Spitz dashed back and forth, the toe of Bones' sock in his mouth, legs pumping as he tried to pull it free. "Ester, help."

Essence sighed beside me, then jumped down, her socked feet sliding on the floor. "Tiger," she called, her voice the firmest I'd heard from her, "come here. Papa Bonesy, he's not scawwy."

Bones froze in place, and I smiled at him. She'd called him papa without being asked, telling him she'd absorbed the messages he'd given, both from his lips and from his heart. He was her home, like he was mine.

Chapter Six

Bones

"Mason." Bones leaned in and gripped the back of his brother's neck, holding him close for a moment. "It has been too long."

It was Christmas day, and the party at the clubhouse had been a success. Ester and Plowboy had secured a present for every child under fifteen that matched both need and personality, and Bones had been amazed again and again at his woman's powers of observation.

"Tell me, brother." Mason's eyes were shining, and Bones understood what he asked. "I hear you found a solution that couldn't be more perfect."

"Truth, my friend." He turned and his gaze unerringly went to where Essence was playing with the other children. "She is quiet, but not more than one might expect." He shook his head. "She is quietly perfect.

And Ester, oh my God, Mason. So much change. All for the better and with no strain. None at all. This is not my woman trying to be something she is not. This is a woman coming into her own because a child depends on her."

"How long has she been with you now?" Mason passed him a beer and Bones took it, scanning the crowd to see Ester seated next to Bella, her eyes also on Essence.

"Ester? She has been in my life for longer, but with me for nearly three years." He shook his head. "Hard to believe. On the one hand, it seems just yesterday we lost Watcher and the other men, but on the other, I feel Ester has always been with me."

"You were frantic to find her." Bones nodded. Not something he'd ever tried to deny, the need to have Ester safe. "You gonna be a bear with the girl, too?"

Laughing, Bones said, "Probably true. Still, I find myself checking on her at night. It has been two weeks, but I count her breaths in the darkness. How do you do it with an infant? She will be five in days, and I cannot imagine the fear that would cloak me if she were so dependent."

"Worth every minute, though." Mason slung an arm around Bones' neck. "Slate's here, you see him yet?" Bones shook his head. "He's got another one on the way."

"No. Tell me this is not multiples. Tell me he did not gift Ruby with a third set of twins?" Looking around, he caught sight of Slate near the door, arm protectively around his Ruby, a petite woman with flaming red hair and a softly rounded belly. "I am glad he came."

"He wouldn't have if the child hadn't landed on your doorstep. Respecting the challenges, he and Ruby had already decided to stay home."

Bones was stunned into silence, then shook his head. "Damn. There are times, you know, when I forget how much love we all have for the other. He would have cut himself out of this, a chance to see old friends, to keep from hurting my woman."

"Brothers, man. We always, always have each other's backs."

The lights from the enormous Christmas tree reflected off the walls, and in the glow, he saw Ester's head turn his direction. Knowing her eyes were on him, he smiled broadly, then mouthed an "I love you" to her. She slumped towards Bella, their heads together, and he heard Ester's bright laughter.

"I have never been this happy, Mason." Holding up his beer, he waited until Slate made his way over, then clinked rims with him, then Mason, followed quickly by Shades and Red, and Tater, until he'd acknowledged them all. Every man who formed this close circle was his brother beyond the patch. His ride-or-die friends, the ones he counted on to have his back time and again, as Mason had said.

"Rebels forever," Bones began the familiar refrain, pride filling his chest when every voice in hearing range picked it up, ending it. "Forever Rebels."

Dear Reader – I find myself at a loss for words fit to convey the depth of gratitude I carry in my soul for all of you. It is true Mica *began this journey for me, and* Christmas Doings *will likely end the RWMC part of this path we walk together. Love her or hate her, if it weren't for that green-eyed chick, we wouldn't be here right now. But, if it weren't for you? Well, let's just say I owe you everything. So much love, respect, and honor for you. See you in another book!* ~ML

THANK YOU SO MUCH FOR READING
CHRISTMAS DOINGS!

I truly hoped you enjoyed this story in the RWMC family saga. Thanks for taking this trip along with me.

~ML

ABOUT THE AUTHOR

Raised in the south, MariaLisa learned about the magic of books at an early age. Every summer, she would spend hours in the local library, devouring books of every genre. Self-described as a book-a-holic, she says "I've always loved to read, but then I discovered writing, and found I adored that, too. For reading...if nothing else is available, I've been known to read the back of the cereal box."

Also by MariaLisa deMora

Neither This, Nor That MC Series

Legends are born from moments like these. Folktales spun around a single point in time so perfect, you can almost hear the click resonating through the universe as things align. Meet Twisted, Po'Boy, Retro, and Ragman, good old boys from southern states who have many things in common.

First, is a bone-deep love of the biker lifestyle.

Second, would be their love of the brotherhood, and knowing that you trust the man at your back.

Finally, these men have the love of a good woman. None of these come without a price, and it is our pleasure to journey along with them as they discover the blessings that can be won, and lost along the way.

Raving Reviews for NTNT book one:
This is the Route of Twisted Pain

"*This is the Route of Twisted Pain* is an exhilarating, gripping romance novel contrived of incredible world building, complex yet relatable characters, and a unique, captivating plot.

Gifted storyteller MariaLisa deMora beautifully balances exciting suspense, fast action, intriguing secrets with delicious, blazing hot romance scenes.

Readers will be up all night with this riveting page-turner."

~NY Literary Magazine

"Bloody superb ... as beautiful deep as it is
hot, romantic, and fierce."

~Becky Johnson
Executive director and CEO, Hot Tree Editing

"Getting a book that gives you that all-encompassing,
can't put it down, want to live in that world feeling is
the holy grail for a reader
and this book has that."

~Miranda J.
Mommy's a Book Whore

"This story has it all. Enough drama to keep you hooked,
enough spice to light you up, and an incredible amount
of emotion that just seems to pour off the pages."

~Erin B.
FMR Book Grind

"It's addictive and exciting as you travel the route of
twisted pain. It's an experience you do not want to
miss."

~Rosa S
iScream Books

"I loved this book and the characters so much. I can't
wait for more of the Incoherent MC."

~Marie
Naughty Moms' Story Time

"Theirs was an all encompassing love ready to stand together and at times stand for each other."
~She Heart's Books

"There are a lot of things that I could say about this book: The plot? Exceptional. The sex? Some of the best I've ever read. The characters? Impressive. This Is The Route Of Twisted Pain has every ingredient of a great book but you know what REALLY makes this an extraordinary book? The words. MariaLisa deMora has an uncanny talent for evoking your senses with words. You feel every. single. one."
~Jamey W.
Confessions of a Serial Reader

"This is not your typical love story but let me tell you this is how a love story should be. ... I would give this book TEN stars if I could. Can't wait for the next installment of the Neither This, Nor That series."
~Kylee

"This may be the best book I read all year. These people...they're not characters, they're real... have stuck in my head from the day I met them. MariaLisa deMora can throw words down that'll Twist (hehe) your insides up till you can't breathe for waiting to hear what's next!"
~DeLane C

"I enjoyed the ever-loving-heck out of This Is the Route of Twisted Pain."
~Angela G.
Wicked Reads

"I love MariaLisa and the way she weaves a story!"

~G.M. Scherbert

Author

"This is a wild, gritty ride and I loved every moment of it. I was hooked from the first page and madly in love with 'Twisted' George Bell by the end of the first chapter…I devoured this story in a single afternoon and fell in love with a new to me author before I'd finished this first book. I love the characters, I love Twisted's world and I can't wait for the next book."

~Sarah

Wicked Reads

"Fantastic!!! This story drew me in from the very beginning and held me on the edge to the very end. MariaLisa deMora did a great job setting the tone from the very beginning. Penny was one of the best heroines I've ever met. She was absolutely fearless! I can't wait to read the next book in the series."

~Rose

"First off, let me state that there was one thing I didn't like about this book and that is the LAST PAGE! I hated for it to end. I dearly loved this book and its characters as well as their setting. Thank you dear authoress. I am a very happy reader for having been so entertained whist living vicariously through the lives of the characters in this book. It is indeed; a book I'll reread many times down the road."

~Colleen M

"I was pulled into this story from the very beginning and couldn't put it down. The dishes, laundry, housework all got put on hold until I could finish this book. This is first book from MariaLisa and certainly won't be my last."

~LeAnn F
Cherry O Blossoms Promotions

"... it's so dirty, dirty hot!!"

~Melissa M.
Alpha Book Club

ADDITIONAL SERIES AND BOOKS

Please note that books in a series frequently feature characters from additional books within that series. If series books are read out of order, readers will twig to spoilers for the other books, so going back to read the skipped titles won't have the same angsty reveals.

Neither This, Nor That series:

This Is the Route Of Twisted Pain, #1
Treading the Traitor's Path: Out Bad, #2
Trapped by Fate on Reckless Roads, #3
Shelter My Heart, #4

Rebel Wayfarers MC series:

Mica, #1
A Sweet & Merry Christmas, short story #1.5
Slate, #2
Bear, #3
Jase, #4
Gunny, #5
Mason, #6

Hoss, #7
Harddrive Holidays, short story #7.5
Duck, #8
Biker Chick Campout, short story #8.5
Watcher, #9
A Kiss to Keep You, novella #9.25
Gun Totin' Annie, short story #9.5
Secret Santa, novella #9.75
Bones, #10
Gunny's Pups, novella #10.25
Never Settle, short story #10.5
Not Even A Mouse, novella #10.75
Fury, #11
Christmas Doings, #11.25
Gypsy's Lady, #11.5
Cassie, #12
Road Runner's Ride, novella #12.5

Occupy Yourself band series:

Born Into Trouble, #1
Grace In Motion, #2 (TBD)
What They Say, #3 (TBD)

Other Books:

With My Whole Heart
Alace Sweets
Hard Focus

More information available at mldemora.com.

www.ingramcontent.com/pod-product-compliance
Lightning Source LLC
Chambersburg PA
CBHW061252170626
46809CB00007B/2958